DAS' INDIFFERENCE

J. B. JACOB

ISBN 979-888555361-2

Contents

CHAPTER ONE

INTRODUCTION TO INDIFFERENCE

I sit here all day like a stubbed and burnt-up cigar bud, on this orthodox leather chair in half-ruins, silently waiting in patience for the whistling mid-night breeze to come and sweep away these crushed ashes of last night's passionless reveries into my undercooked, bruised history. This is my new, refined life. This is my last attempt at glory. The porcelain, make-shift candle holder stands good by the vernacular, wind-oppressed windows. It is post-lunch period.

The best of prose have spilled from unfulfilled ambitions. I have no regrets, in whatever that could be categorised under the iconic heading of "so far", and in all that is yet to be, all the great wavery decisions I am about to undertake. You'll know. Nothing much. Nothing much is all I have, all a rusted, untuned string could afford in this life and the most beautiful and best of other lives contained within the scope of a stretched and expansive bracket.

Contained.

Surrounded by an unsorted circle of working men, comprised mostly of the elderly and the naturally indifferent, now and then I stare with a blank heart at the scorching laptop monitor in front, plainly to escape these off-seasonal judgements and lunch-time whispers. Of all, that cold, collective gaze, unbearable and tremendous.

Only if I could decipher my real intentions, the true psychology behind the random and unmotivated actions, and, if there are, any logical reasoning for unprecedented absurdities.

There is something else, I am pretty sure. Something less intense, lesser orderly; for there is much order in this new, stripped world let me go take a good sleep.

I wake up from a short-lived nap, nothing much has changed, yet change accustoms as the sole proprietor of the informal flow, the conventional seminary maids serve me chicken rice for early dinner, and I take a few steps forward. I come across an appearance of slight wonder, one of Keats' joy. I gaze at this little beauty-carrier and a question has been raised, obviously in regard to its magnificence and its awesome origin. A line is drawn and in it contained the thing and the beauty, mingled inseparably like a Colgate tooth-paste, the curious question raised, me, Keats', my eternal rival James Joyce, my another persistent, picturesque rival Steve Mccurry, unsorted men, the Colgate paste, the line itself. Which one of the lot is superior, and which of them has more relevance, also very nicely erodes and slides down, slowly, into the pit of that classic, epic line.

Ambani too.

“This reality is a mere passing appearance, screeched and exaggerated and dramatic - an expressive extension, if the consideration is turned the other way round. The key of choice has already been arranged for the enthusiastic opener,” - *me.*

Dead chicken, strangely enough, impressively excites the curious, amateurish soul.

It is provoking to know that this is the only being I'll ever have. As per the current goings, I guess so.

When we were young we were addicted. Me and my brother. Like owned metals in controlled magnetic fields, within the rough and hardy coats of Tommy Vercetti of a pirated, abridged version of Miami or Los Angeles, we used to drift across the splendid wonders of vintage vibes. And once thoroughly induced in its addictive thrills, a mutual reverberation was certainly implied, for the controller soon melted and blended with the modified reality under control.

That is all melancholic installations of distractive characteristics from the past. What use now!

I have truly become that amateurish wannabe whom I conceived few months back for some pocket money and glorious press meets. Then I didn't know what I was slipping into; today, I am stripped flat naked in the endless void. Before touching the divine granite marbles of deeper dread, on my way here, on that violet, bulky car of my brother's distilled morality, vacantly stuck in a restless traffic block as the old driver detestably cursed the unsystematic nature of the people of this swiftly developing land, my endless gaze was aimlessly relaxed on the crowded pale leaves of a vaguely remembered road-side suspended tree. It was the golden hour and my natural gaze turned impressionistic; there, at that very moment of undirected tranquillity, I had proudly claimed to have experienced the phenomenological truth of my broken existence. Yes, it happened to me out of nowhere; out of the empty leather seats or my endless gaze or the glowing images. Wherever it may have gloriously hid. Later, I realised I was just floating flat in negative voids.

I had been carrying this burden of existence for some time now. On my way to the tapioca plantations or my neighbour's paddy fields, through the slowly unfolding nights and over the backyard greens, my overflowing reveries now and then tripped uncontrollably at the thought of this inescapable weight unnecessarily hanging on my shoulders. I could have perhaps thrown all of it away and walked a free path like a normal rational. But then I would again slide back into those sophisticated evening meets and pretentious conversations, those classic gossip sessions around lavish party tables in refined county clubs that were once so very dear to me and lay close by my youthful, throbbing heart. So I guess it is better this way; to bleed mildly in endless gazes than dress in make-believes that could turn highly flammable in time.

Gazes.

I didn't start writing to describe any of these tasteless observations (not the paragraph above but the one above that!) or evidently glorify any of my claims by merely stating them; I resorted to typing abstract notes again, solely to escape time. And these getaway moments are what have been translated into white letters.

'Active writing' is what my refreshed mind often tend to refer to these fragmented bits of abrupt and spontaneous notes that are basically on free roam mode. So at this very moment, at the tip of my accelerating thumps, I baptise myself on carefree prose and roasted nuts and emerge out as Das Rajan. Here I am, nailed in the whirling headache of a confusing phase, as occasional as a broiler chicken, checked upon purely on humanitarian sake and dialled upon either accidentally or out of sheer necessity, or in rare scenarios, within elongated hours of anxiety strikes. These words may be too polished and exaggerated to digest, but it is sadly true, as *irreal* yet splendid as that white butterfly that just flew away into the overloaded indistinctness of the backyard garden - neglected and autonomous.

Thirty-eight hard and solitary years it took for the great Joseph Conrad to realise that some men are not equipped with fortunes of life; only existence few have in possession, cold and heavy, like the wavering rains and early nights of November.

November.

It was perhaps on one such cold November night that I flew to the Gulf from my hometown's dwarf airport, leaving behind my young and caring wife and the sprouting children, whose brand new, slightly flawed faces I can now retrace on the black sandpapers of my imagination only by rough and blurred approximations. As I get in terms with this hard, deeply upsetting fact, I sincerely pray to the Gods beyond that they will one day forgive me for who I have been, for all I have done.

Perhaps not.

Oh.

Looking back at those engaging, reverberating business days in Bahrain and occasional first class official trips to Kuwait and Abu Dhabi, let me be frank, my restless heart still trembles in fear. What was the uncontrollable rush and formal encounters all about? What have I ultimately gained except for this tropical misery and periodical bursts of regrets? Only if she could understand and shine a little light into the dark caves where I am now secretly lodged from debtors and scary media persons.

In reality, Deepa Paulose is the only sensible person I have ever come across in this very short span of my compressed and further degrading timeline. But the ontological sticks holding her fluctuated temperaments is far too deep rooted in aristocratic household values that there is not much she could do for me now. By that I mean reunite in another ceremonious ring-exchange of course. Impossible, I know it is. But nobody can stop my imagination from roaming around purposelessly in unchartered territories like an unguided flight before take-off.

People are dispersing around me like herds of sheep left unattended; they are returning home, only to come back tomorrow and repeat the same process again and again in endless, monotonous loops. When will all of them realise this hard core fact that the meaning of life is to come in terms with this ruthless, tiring monotony they are all so collectively trying to run away from? Well, who am I to judge! I too had my days. Tense and on the edge days. Ah! They have all turned to black as my days have become darker than nights.

An undecipherable green fruit had fallen from the widespread tree in the backyard, reuniting with its fellow siblings after temporary moments of unavoidable separation. Beyond the dense, rather narrow and intersectional branches of this low, crouching tree near the humming backyard basketball court beyond the outhouse premises that I am currently positioned under in absence of running thoughts or flashback loops, blurred leaves keep slightly trembling in accordance to the whistle of the travelling winds and local birds on lowered flights. On my way through the dark and shady corridors of the bricked primary school building - whose huge compound and cornered extension of an isolated, possessed-looking outhouse is my passing monthly home for the night, shades of dim red thrown on the pinkish walls by the sinking sun seize my attention and fulfil my senses as the sound of approaching footsteps upon nearing the outhouse front-yard of fallen leaves and slippery tiles and overgrown grass made my delicate heart slightly quake. It is the Reverend. His worn, swollen eyes got tightly attached to the slender and exaggerated compositions of dried leaves of a rather short date palm near the porch. As soon as his other, parallel senses deciphered the incoming approach of my dimmed figure, he had his composure quickly retrieved from aesthetic appreciations and had his attentive gaze pulled back. His cotton mask was hanging on his neck like the good old Tambourine Man's harmonica.

"Good evening, Father. What a pleasant hour of the day it is!" greeted I, pleasingly, with great reverence as my searching hands impatiently pulled out from the pockets a surgical mask and had it fixed on my moist face; it was a simple show of deep respect for old age.

"Good evening, Mr. Rajan," replied the old priest, stiffly, with a reserved smile suspended on his wrinkled face. "Indeed it is, young man. Sunsets on top of hills are always heart-warming. Hope you are having a wonderful time here," said he in gentler tones. He had been softened of the initial toughness and was becoming friendlier and welcoming. At least, that's what I noted from the fluctuations in his reactions.

"Oh, all good, Father! The view of the hills from my room is fantastic!," I laid out in elated excitement.

The Reverend responded with an immediately occurred smile and turned his gaze to the tiled grounds; recent rains had the painted tiles buried in autumnal leaves, a mix of both tiny and usual ones. The security guards in blue or the women in colourful *saris* had forgotten to sweep the dry, wet leaves away. The splendid sight of fallen leaves below my knees failed to distract me from the instantaneous anxiety felt from within; somehow this peaceful awkwardness needs to be cut. Something needs to be done without further delay.

"Father..," for a moment I searched for words; or perhaps it was an evident lack of proper framework in my thoughts. "Did you enquire about the matter I had requested?" I finally pulled out the clogged words that got plugged in a mesh of thoughts.

After foggy moments of confused search and careful analysis, gradual projections of uneasiness and trouble became tangible in the scholarly, 20th century face as the senior-most pastor of the House strenuously tilted his gaze from below to confront a mysterious glow in my anxious eyes; the previously observed indifference or reservation had completely vanished from his now bemused eyes. I sensed another incoming tragedy. My mind has over the years been trained specifically in decoding tragedies, for they came in plenty and at the most unexpected, awkward places.

"Oh, yes, I did enquire about it today morning, Mr. Rajan. I had completely lost hold of in the daily rush. I am getting old, you see," replied he, retrospectively. "Tell me, Das. Do have any prior teaching experiences?" He asked, seriously. "Because I had a chat with the Director of the school after breakfast regarding any vacancies and he says that at the moment, as you are very well aware of the current dire circumstances, there aren't any openings for teacher roles. 'Dear Reverend,' he told me with a helpless face, 'We are in fact overloaded with the current staff'," thus did the Reverend speak in exceptional frankness, in the meanwhile showing-off his imitative skills.

Very much expecting another random rejection that my current under-goings have been revolving around and getting used to in the meantime, I was in fact surprisingly taken aback by this sudden turn of events, for in my mind preparations for celebration and after parties had already commenced; even after these many years of misfortunes and countless self-reflections, this wretched infinitely hopeful item in me will never learn the harsh fundamentals of life, that the fortunes it carries entitles my name in delayed expectations.

"Oh, is that so," I replied, dimly, pretending to be absorbed. "I actually have no teaching experience as such. But once I used to run a coaching centre in Gulf, where nursing students were given vocational skills training and basic lessons in foreign languages by me and my wife and one of our mutual friend," enthusiastically I added after a short pause.

"You were in the Gulf," exclaimed the reverend in astonishment. "What made you leave the Middle-East? My younger brother's both grandsons are settled in Dubai. And, yeah, they earn a lot, I tell you. The Middle-East is the right place if you have the will and the determination that one should by default carry along with his passport to be able to survive the strict environment," he said, casually, having become in terms and accommodative of my harmless standing-by status.

"Yes. I was in the Gulf during the time of extreme springs," and so did I begin my short speech summarising the whole of my strange, dramatic life in the gulf so far, up to this desperate point of pleading for work, knocking at every visible, available door. Debt; struggle; heavy days; longer nights; roti and white sauce; loneliness; glory; downfall; bankruptcy; international laws; creditors; bounced cheques; sleeping pills; divorce; endless wanderings; philosophy - as our conversation - which had turned more or less an unofficial confession session, gained momentum, I saw myself unfolding and revealing far too much to the theological man by my side, whose distinguished, enlightened presence had made the moving world and my sense of time slip into the neglected, uncredited background, obscured and passive.

Immediate, innocent excitements in expressive contacts with fellow people in itself is a form of spirituality, at the least in mild magnitudes.

In another moment I reckoned myself tramping in thoughtful reflections through the lovely football turf yard below - flattened and exaggerated in front of the seminary building, on the lowered level of the massive campus, with an unsettled mind overflown in whistling thoughts from many directions, for in revisiting those dark days of hardships, glory and horror, I had fallen yet again into the shapeless pit of regrets that I have been trying to escape thereafter. Children from the neighbouring houses were cycling and playing hide and seek by the open space near the turf, and they bowed down to us in appreciable manners as the white lights from the adjacent lamp posts cast lengthy shadows of the high priest on their playful bodies when the former reunited with me in similarly quiet observations on his way down, after having completed an extensive, immersive correspondence with misplaced leaves and wild garden flowers.

And with that our disappointing, twice-repeated encounters had come to an end; few walkable blocks away was the churchmen's quarters and the reverend, thrusting hard on his glossy and wooden walking stick, slowly proceeded alone to the whitewashed building, leaving me behind lost and distorted like an accidental downpour.

The reverend disappeared into panoramic dimness of the closing evening and soon afterwards, while closing the wooden door of my pale room and bolting it and cross-checking its protective efficiency twice, I listened to the stirring of approaching migraines closing in on my temples. Yes, it is here again; after many a good days of order and donated calmness as a result of its uninformed disappearance, it has forced itself upon my freely flowing moods, right at this slow hour before the introductory hours to existentialism. Without adhering to any of its destructive advances, I spend the leftover hours of the day in uninterrupted solitude by the geometric window, crouched in the depths of the creakingly mobile chair and under the vintage appeal of the burning candle by the open window and my denim pants desperately pleaded for recognition; roasting already-prepared nuts in candle fire has become my new time-moving activity, an effective boredom killer free or cost: I'll have to cast melancholic looks of last goodbyes to this temporary home too, much sooner than my analytical senses had initially worked out; a life was unsuspectingly placed and I chose to be completely disaffectionate in its curvy, scrambled swings.

Elaborated, spread-out days; lengthier, sour.

In the morning my after-sleep, yawning consciousness completely shaken by a surprise visit by one of my old acquaintances, Ibrahim Kunnumpuram, with whom I had formed a strong brotherly association in Assam during an absurd yet beautiful short phase of my subjectivist becoming when I was working as a tourist guide in Kaziranga; young and charming, those were the good old days of natural innocence and genuine friendships before ambition swept my life away from me. While shutting the window of my lonesome gazes and sleepless reveries, the tiny marble pot - the one I had articulately stolen from my brother's apartment, fell to the floor in the sweet, caressing touch of the silky curtain, its fine upper portion shattered to the floor. Now placed on the windowsill, half-broken and perspective distorted, this grand crockery piece once contained all my curiosity and affection; each day is another unforeseen low.

Walking down the front lawns towards the breakfast hall, passing through green gates and slippery steps, my wandering mind was suddenly numbed after meeting the excited eyes and thrilled speech of the soulful recurrence from a long forgotten past; people from memories resurface in the strangest manners: Ibrahim and I shook hands, hugged each other for moments, switching shoulders every now and then, like brothers after years of painful separation. Neither of us cared to pull up our masks hanging on our necks; in the heights of prolonged reminiscence, we forgot the moment, the present, the daily blows of existence, the virus lurking outside, for both of us were captivated by the virtual tears descending from the hard days of our shared past. Ibrahim and I, after recovering our certain presence in the present, wore our masks in medically prescribed ways and maintained a specific social distance, and we fulfilled the remaining few steps together, conversing and often bursting into laughters and remembering our good old days filled with youth and hopes.

Ibrahim used to work for a big tea estate lord, as his personal driver and, confidentially, as his most trusted employee, often staying overnight for heavy drinks and secretive, inner talks at his huge bungalow in the border between Assam and Nagaland, spending drunken nights in the comforts of his boss' warm guesthouses that were actually conceived for important persons. Most of the high officials from Kaziranga politely rejected his uncertified invitations stating long distance issues, the hidden reality being the wealthy bachelor's unbearable arrogance. Though Ibrahim himself was subject to insider speculations, he never really adhered to any of its resonances, and not in the least for the drunken abuses mainly because, firstly, the fortune incurred was very strong and, of course, the huge cartons of imported liquor he got for free. So did Ibrahim Kunnumpuram, a man of weak eyes and unpredictable bursts of arrogance himself, son of late sailor, Ahmed Ibrahim,, who died in the eastern seas while on duty, without hesitations or second thoughts accompany his young master through all his misadventures and spirited endeavours. And in one such crazy undertaking did he trip from the rooftop of his neighbour's (in respect to his spare home in Kaziranga) thatched house where he had climbed up effortfully, with utmost care, one drowsy night, for a better view of the massive hill range beyond in moonlit silhouette and on his creaky drop, fortuitously rescue a trapped rattle snake from the assembled straws. As a token of gratitude, the very next day the local committee got together and handed him over the freed venomous snake in a handy cage, and Ibrahim had it safely kept in the trunk of their minivan as his master, baffled and uneasy, drove the car in high speeds through the national highways towards his bungalow on the farther side. Unsure about its coiled future, the venomous species monotonously hissed through the empty spaces between the rusted bars, now and then exposing its forked tongue, bizarre and special.

Back at the off-centred bungalow, though initial thoughts vouched to roast it in the barbecue grill using burning charcoal and serve it as an experimental substitute for fish pickle that on regular days ideally blended with white rum, reflections on morality and, most of all, on the current powerful status of human rights commissions and their wide-reaching, global outlook, his chief ordered Ibrahim to do whatever was necessary to return the snake to the wilderness in the most civilian and respectable manner possible, for in the couple or more solitary days he spend with the spiral-like, highly flexible reptile, the young owner had developed special, sentimental affections with its frightful yet tranquil compositions.

Thus embarked Ibrahim on his return journey to the National Park after spending some friendly days with his master on his bungalow. In the back of the minivan was loaded the sleeping snake, and upon arriving in Kaziranga did the honest young man Ibrahim had to cross unexpected solemn paths with another struggling migrant – a reserved yet outgoing tourist guide, which was none but me, formally marking the beginning of a fine brotherhood defined by strong working class temperaments, until that very cursed moment of avarice explosion on a quiet Sunday evening when I paced down the slope of the native orthodox church, alone and tired, and felt the extreme, perpetual cry from the depths of my impatient, restless heart ringing in my confused head. Couple of weeks, or maybe months thereafter, I don't exactly remember, I abandoned my relatively relaxed job of frequent shuttles in and out the lengthy and massive wilderness of Kaziranga, returned home and spend some essential time with family. Later into the night of a rather difficult and strenuous day in terms of intellectual strength, I packed my bags to the Gulf, to grab in full force and at a wholesale stretch, all of the thrills, sufferings and bad faiths this life could handle. All the downfalls of life I was able to contain to a certain level in suppressed emotions or transcendental leaps until just before, where, in the sloppy down-hill stairs leading to the school's ground level I met him, my good old friend Ibrahim, after these many odd years of forgotten details, whereby all the contained memories burst and spilled in uncontrollable fluidity as though these many years they carried the reality of unattended boiled milk about to pop.

Not much drastic changes were discerned on his visible features in respect to the gone-by years, apart from loss of hygiene and a quietly protruding tummy. When confronted by the local police for casual inspection as our north eastern reminiscences led us in our existential passiveness well into the depths of the empty morning streets, both of us realised with a sigh of revoked pride that our iron bond and general outlook withstood the rusts of time. We found our way back to the lower gate of the school compound with a dragging heart, and Ibrahim, in his turn, earnestly narrated the story of his blessed life, how he abandoned the clutches of his aggressive but compassionate boss and found enormous warmth and spiritual upliftment in the divine hands of the reverend, who was then a young and generous chaplain. It was this loving soul who had retold the unfortunate tale of my pitiful career to Ibrahim and the small assembly of fellow clergymen, local artistes, small-scale traders and other officials who were gathered around the big round-table in the main hall for the weekly reunion breakfast where they discuss regional politics, community development and general philosophy. Minimalistic dishes were served and later, while consuming garden fruit desserts, the reverend, seated without evident objections in the high, leather lone chair in the unclassified intersection of both curves, in order to cut the mild tension in the air due to usual disagreements, began briefly recounting in a very composed manner the story of a struggling young man who fled to the middle east in search of the high life, but after gaining more than what he aimed at, lost balance and fell with a thud into the pit of debts and misery. In the end, before signing off with a moral message, the enlightened soul disclosed the proud fact that this young man - a mutual friend of one of his well-wishers, having self-extracted from the sins of the external world, is decently lodging in the outhouse of the church school until he secures a safe and steady job. When more than necessary personal information were inadvertently revealed as the ageing mind got lost in the flow of words, glowing images of a bygone phase seemed to remerge from buried waters in the imagination of Ibrahim, whose mellow presence too was felt in this circular collection of distinguished persons since, after returning from Kaziranga disowning soft labour, with financial help from his well-off relatives, he opened a pocket sized snap studio and independently learned the basics of photography; in the slow passing of a dry and companionless year, acronyms and bynames associated to artists preceded his initials. Well-off and popular and reputed in the miniature globe of his hilly homeland as the personal photographer of the hills, Ibrahim had travelled a long way from the difficulties of deprivation and odd jobs. Feasting among his own people, chills of wealth and recognition made his tender heart leak in the melancholic mood induced by the reverend's short story and the overflowing of preserved images from the obscure days of his unreflective estimations.

Convinced of the trustful validity of his intuition and fully determined to prove them right, settling the routine affairs with the feasting lot, his speeding legs transcended the polished, psychedelic tiles of the large dining hall and other relative spaces with hurried steps and a vibrating heart, confronting my absent-minded, nature-observant time-pass with spilling joy. And ascending the same steps of chance ecstasies with twinkling eyes and a satisfied mind, I observe closely the withering trees of climate change and the starry gleam in my eyes go dim as I reckon with an emotionally charged smile that though the vintage trees of southern hills turn pale in autumn with a tint of pastel red, they still praise-worthily maintain their elegant physiques. Someone in my head pulled up from transcendental, evolving grounds a transparent placard and held it high in the void-sky: "Life is hard, but it'll always be beautiful," it read and I underwent a sensation of blue and emotional attractions that was beyond subjectivism and open to all. For a moment I paid a silent tribute to Jean-Paul Sartre, to Dhirubhai Ambani, to Vincent Van Gogh, and all the great auteurs and industrialists who sincerely faced, survived and triumphed this waterlogged ontology. Turning my emotional gaze from the white, cloud-filled skies to the sprouting grounds, like Princy piercing into Robert's affectionate eyes, I looked deep into my thoughts and whispered, 'Gratitude, Princy. A thousand gratitude.

The scene gone over-the-top.

I hastily hurried to my room through the golden porch of November bliss and threw myself onto its stuffy emptiness just a few minutes ago.

Entering the dim, pale room of yellowish curtains and cemented walls and cold floors, I blankly waited till midnight for sleep to come. Before it finally arrived drawing drowsy patterns in my dreamy mind, my endless gaze into the blue night was interrupted with a quick peak into the crumbled white paper Ibrahim had handed me over before us exchanging compact, hearty handshakes. In it was scribbled in faint blue impressions directions to the excavation site Ibrahim was assigned to document as a photographic series, and to which I was cordially invited as a spectator friend. Mild delights, however futile or tedious, was still left in my time.

CHAPTER TWO

ARCHAEOLOGICAL EXCAVATIONS

By ten the sun was scorching high and dispersed and, a large group, including the documentation crew, archaeological excavation team and other officials in-charge were circled around a huge and penetrating stone well in half-ruins that was very recently discovered - unearthed from eroded grounds with the aid of a primeval, revived map. There were all sorts of people - researchers, scholars, documentarians, officials, historical enthusiasts, guards, daily-wage workers, diggers, passers-by, excited onlookers, premium visitors: in general, a brownish hallucination, ancient and dizzying.

If I had the slightest of hints about the tiresome length of the day-in-hand in advance, I would have stayed home and listened to the rumbling of the ceiling fan or stare endlessly at the silhouettes of the sculptors working outside forming amorphous figures on the yellow curtains, frequently alternating in accordance to the migrating winds or movements. Now that I am here, my slippery mind keeps drifting uneasily, always dragging behind me like a trained pet, forming obscure patterns and shadowy figures from the medieval period or beyond in the great cavities of the deep well. Amidst a crowd after so long, unintentionally becoming part of the accidental mob, I took extra care not to glide too far into any of my imaginary outings, for many a times have my good old friends warned me against bizarre bodily movements and abrupt laughters which often were categorised as social embarrassments.

Slowly sliding past the crowd to the upper grounds of untamed green, shortly afterwards I saw myself immersed in meaningless walks through antique woods faraway on the other side of the ancient, naturally preserved land, and in a matter of minutes, saw Ibrahim, whose sincere attention was trapped in the narrowed view-finder of his mirrorless camera that was steadily devoted at a cryptic inscription engraved on a carved granite stone somewhere beyond the woods. Subsequently I was met by his driving gaze, and after shaking hands and exchanging few friendly words, I was introduced to the head of the whole documentation business, his boss of the day who, after having inwardly studied his charming attitude and manipulative talks, seemed a man of high influence.

Thereby cautiously maintaining a plain distance in order not to avoid any complications (you never know the thoughts that circle around busy, restless heads), and having spent some brief, awkward moments with the semi white-collar workers and the busy Ibrahim, I peeled greenish oranges and consumed their bittersweet essence under the lonesome shade of a crouching tree. The sun was tilting higher, and the shades shrunk exponentially. Unable to contain my floating thoughts and lost in gone-by images, I again took to my feet and resumed to stroll through the woods like a highly transparent fluid. There were women in nighties plucking berries and picking fallen leaves; a man in torn vests was cutting wood, greatly exposing his side muscles; and I, as a-lonesome as always, must have been gazing on the wild grounds looking for hidden snakes or undiscovered gold.

An hour or more must have drove by in solitary musings around the union of pine trees and other wild plants, and extremely tired of the tremendous heat and repetitive figures and reveries, out on the busy streets which was moving completely in disregard to the current health crisis, the idle stretched-out posture of a green river beyond a curving road turned my soul blue: at the split of a second that was in immediate reflections paused and elaborated, I realised that I am after all living - that all of this, the great sufferings, comfortable loneliness, agony, the unbearable heat or leaking happiness, consists in or of this much-celebrated life that is often being talked about, most of the times taken for granted, sometimes to the point of glorification or incomprehensible philosophy. This is existence, I am living: in every passable and impermanent details and nuts and bolts a bare glimpse of me, rusted or shiny, flowed on ceaselessly and I saw in them nothing but myself. Or, perhaps, I am mistaken. I have altered my words and my thoughts, perhaps I witness in myself something that is essentially and indefinable more than me yet still graspable; in glimpses and in occasions it occurs to be an arm's distance away yet never reachable. In May it is me and when it rains the soil erodes and slides away; peculiar and especial. Better still, I find it in me when the sun turns low and clumsy at six and then there is the season of leaving home.

For all the past splendours and great triumphs and grant victories, and all the upcoming tragedies of human conditions, well, contained and constrained within this moment of private reflections that is solely mine, jogging away so effortlessly in respect to its own personalised and inapproachable laws. Passing-by men dauntingly stared at my grungy, nonchalant dressing, and their endless gazes made a hole through my white walls of resistance, awakening my suppressed angsts. Some have been fastened for far too long in reality they need to get out sometimes to really get to know about its fullness.

Existence Jr.

Abandoning the image of the great river that had now turned saturated in hues of dark blue after a swamp of clouds having buried the microwave sun, and after discomfortable operations with a roadside shopkeeper who refused me cigarettes citing health concerns for my relatively young age (no, not because I was under-aged or my relative appearances in any showed any sign of that - just that he was the usual deeply caring sort-of guy) - which did raise my motivation levels after a very long time, and after these light encounters with the fast-paced, well-fed reality, I eagerly told myself, “All is not lost yet,” as I again ascended the steep towards the archaeological land with a can of soft drink in my hand and deep, mingling shades of blue stuck in my tongue while pondering over thenew direction my upcoming existential roam should pursue next. Soft drinks in can costs more than the ones contained in bottles - a quantitative absurdity. What more, the stall-runner in front of the excavation site entrance charged three bucks as “heritage conservation levy,” whatever that would mean. “Did he fool me?” “Am I so easy a target?”

Not all was lost indeed. Though Ibrahim got lost in work, quiet walks through the ancient glory in ruins revealed to me a thing or two about human nature; wherever in space or time, few men always wanted to stand out, and sadly enough, with embarrassment in my recent looks, did I include my own name into this ever-expanding, non-stop list.

A middle-aged man in a red-blue striped t-shirt, dark and faded, that proudly represented the golden years of football in Barcelona, as though on a regular drift through a sloppy countryside or a classic thermometer on downhill drive, was subsiding down the precisely-slashed underground steps of the deep unearthed well that were perfectly carved out within the radius of the pale rock well, thanks to the strenuous efforts of some ancient manual workers in return for few silver nickels or more. Fellow workers looking down the deep pit vaguely shouted and threw in ungraspable gestures directions to their chief, but the latter’s dropping operations mostly rested on timeless, in-house instincts. For after having successfully reached the sunlight-forbidden pit of the deep ancient well, almost an hour went by in continuous toil undertaken by the now minimised, microscopic figure. Ceaselessly he brushed with a whisk broom the untouched bottom of the dry, dehydrated well that was till then submerged in classic mud, eroded soil and contemporary cobwebs, and, in the indecisive, highly flexible passing of the very same hour, my dreamy gaze perpetually shifted focus between the mythical-like ruined walls of the well, its corresponding dark and blurry foundations and the sunburnt and spoiled skies above when, suddenly, rather abruptly, a rather greatly excited shout from downstairs reached our lost-in-our-own-respective-world senses in faint, dispersed waves. It was the chief worker down there. He must have discovered something exceptional and hidden got bitten by a preserved, immortalised dragon. God forbade me! A couple or more repetitive exclamations from deep below, and that was all it took for the dreamy, weary lot above to file together the indistinct resonances and shattered echoes into a combined folder such as "there is a second well here." Exclamation marks reigned here. Deep below, more hard mud was wiped aside, and gaining some sort of super energy, the thick man accelerated his sweeping pace in quick progression, employing all of his might to clean up the underground radius to satisfy his curious imagination feeding on rotten spirits, empty spaces, or by the grace of God, buried gold. Overhead we waited anxiously, fully prepared to catch all the thrown words before they lose whole of their essence in dimensional escalations. Three men took precautionary measures to descend down the earthly steps in calculated degrees, but creaking noises of something opening and a flash of pure, dim blue glare halted their conscious motion midway, altering their invisible steps to blissful stillness. The built man with his natural workman's muscles held high in the tight air the heavy, rusted lid of the rather narrow shielded well, as the three men above and those further above gazed in amazement the low resonance and slight stirring - very spontaneous and unbroken, like jammed automobiles snailing in moderate traffic, of preserved waters stimulating below in slow motion. So pellucid and meditative, the blue reflective waters must have originated before the beginning of time and should necessarily transcend beyond eternity. Lost in the sublime appearance of the pure frame, for a moment all of us stood drugged-still, contemplating on the concealed view, that the shrivelled voice of a work-sight assistant inviting for lunch briefly dodged our melting senses. In imposed remembrances, I was seen bidding suggestive farewells to a surreal world of fellow treasure seekers.

Red chairs encircled adjoined wooden tables like ripened oranges weighing down pregnant citrus trees, and we had our delayed lunch served in palm leafs under the shade of a rampant tree whose thick branches extended upwards towards the intense skies while its gloomy leaves spread horizontally above the silhouetted land, flat and depressed. Ibrahim and I, seated next to each other, lavishly boasted of our heroic operations in rescuing trapped venomous snakes from rooftops, pig sheds or low garages, and in essential interludes, of our misadventures in the wilderness of the famous, concentrated national park too. When we broke into abrupt laughters, the whole team of documentarians and other officials too launched side chuckles or suppressed giggles because, most of them being indoor staffs and desked employees, found it rather bewildering to react to the mysterious strangeness that our misadventures were; few more ounce of casual talk and extended moments of personal introduction would have torn open the empty-wallet misery that I was. So I refrained from indulging too deep into my own tragic melodrama and instead, without notice, put on a deep face in absorbed silence, for my ego was very much entertained and content by the polite bows and formal addressing.

It may have been my own withering self instead, after all these years of humiliation and self-loathe, discreetly getting out the self-made cave to finally feel the sun. Unfortunately, it was raining outside, and the submissive sun was covered in mist and blurred in the harsh raindrops, for the egoistic boss intervened, rigorously surveying my general outlook and repeatedly inquiring about fundamental credentials, and I, after a brief encounter with decay and corrosion, dejectedly returned back to my cave of withdrawal, feeling finished for evermore. Lunch ended in self-conscious table-mannerisms, and I again resorted to effortful leg-wheels under the sun. When the tremendous heat from above turned my throat a coastal desert, and when my hurling spit revealed shades of mild red before landing on the overgrown grounds, the age-old sensation I have been running away from seemed to have resurfaced without warning - the alarming concept of direct encounters with the end.

As I zoomed-in critically into the depths of my dissolving splitter now glittering in shades of soft green, my drowsy mind, already showing signs of extreme weariness under the fierce sun, hesitantly admitted to the careless judgement made few moments before, for my dispelled spit lay on the wild leaves as transparent as the high skies; what was previously discerned as pure blood must have been a heedless mistake, or perhaps some sort of weird play of splitting lights, but in that moment, in that very moment that has now been dissolved safely into the mystical clouds of incurred memories, what was hazily conceived as narrow traces of life-syrup, will go on existing as one, unfiltered and mistaken.

With all these fictional images and deep thoughts whirling around my semi-conscious mind like a running washing machine, with a touch of bitterness I ultimately decided to give upon my free roam mode and lay to temporary rest my aching, complaining legs by a narrow strip of autumnal footsteps not so far away from the unearthed well, for all the fading leaves fallen on the former's cracked tiles half-buried it from the unconfined eyes of drifters and onlookers. An untraceable hour like eternity must have gone with the imaginary, and still perched on that same sweat-stained spot like a street-ridden lamp post, perhaps with notable spatial discrepancies of an inch or more here and there, the chance encounter with the least expected person on that lonesome steps, as shall shortly be narrated with only carefully drawn exaggerations, turned out to be a moment of pure chance that possessed rare yet simple potentials to alter the course of my future wheels, as shall later be revealed in segmentary unfolding.

Wise men and slaves of intelligence spare no lost soul, for this glowing-white bearded man in awesome formal attires and a deep blue panama hat walking down the crackling steps of dry leaves to the wild pathways below, having conversed with me for very brief, spontaneous moments here on this unswept outdoor stairway to wherever it may lead, must have had his blurred semi-consciousness abruptly reactivated, illuminated with an inner spark by the lonesome view of my daytime weariness, for he conveyed spectacular visions in simple dialects in response to my calm and relaxed composure. Let me not unnecessarily interrupt the easy flow of these white expanses with unnecessary introduction scenes, but this old man of sharpened facial hairs and perceptions and blue eyes that sparkled according to the drifting clouds filled the last missing blocks of my mirrorless pale life; every new dawn, and all the sudden twists and turns of my murky roads now impresses to be defined by yet another scribbled address, this time springing from the tip of a wrinkled, time-worn hand:

prasadc@gmail.com

"Write to him, he is an old acquaintance of mine; you seem a good fit for his outwardly simple and qualitatively high living. Write to him, he is a fine fellow. He has been living in the disconnected sereneness of the Nilgiris for so long that he almost owns it. When he was young, he came to me as a disciple; on his return I had my bags packed to follow his unprepared paths but not the courage" spoke the old, greyish beard in gloom-struck, recollective tones after handing me over a folded paper and taking his leave with patient steps, and I, lost in the floating world of the hilly and metaphysical mysteries and wonders awaiting me in the Nilgiris, hung on to the white sheet like a revived lover and unknowingly sunk into its depths, transcending beyond the faint blue to a speculative land of cold mornings, wild berries,, evening reveries and midnight roams.

The lit elation reminded me of that rainy day in October when a random, chance-based taxi and its driver, an economy seat and an uncertain future was awaiting for my slow emergence through the curtained doorway of our ancestral home, as I hurriedly tightened my neck tie and kissed last goodbye to an unresponsive, expressionless wife and two shoulder-hanging children. Then, I was boiling in youthful fantasies; today, stripped of my early uninterrupted sleeping hours, only calculated steps and revised decisions were permitted inside my new outhouse of modest aspirations. The huge, dark figure of of vintage mysticism blurred away into the depths of a palm tree union far ahead, gently dissolving in their green majesty, and the day, already enhanced and overgrown with archaeological delights and aspirations, seemed already over and done with for me; the rest is nothing more than end credits unrolling and elevating from below, regardless of the high gravitational pull, and because of my great attention for needless details, I comfortably relapsed on the reclining couch and stared into the vacuum of the big screen, subtly eyeing the leaving crowd, and patiently waiting for my own turn to leave after the screen fades to complete blackness or nothingness re-interpreted. Until then, I have my moving time thrusted entirely on these footsteps, and until then, my over-speeding mind respectfully adheres to agitation in expectation - for Ibrahim, sealed envelopes from a *khaki*-uniformed postman, for a return journey to the stuffy, candle-lit room, for whatever the damn I have been waiting for all these damned years. An agitation in expectation, slow, bristling and burned.

The remaining hours of the day felt less intense and light hearted, and I took it in a passive, secondary spirit. After having exceeded the time limit allotted for the hour, the calming-down sun went into hiding behind a company of elitist clouds that filled and jubilated the blue skies. As I carefully inserted the scribbled paper back into the tight denim pockets after holding onto the excessively emotional pleasure it offered for long, and delightedly completing the remaining steps in a trailing manner, vague hopes of a philosophical death livened my awakened aspirations that was formerly supposed to have been considered smashed and defeated in an unfortunate tragedy back in the yellow lands: a thousand intellectual mourners and fellow contemporary philosophers stood in faint silences encircling my transcending body of declining health and abundant intellectual success. Well aware of the despairing consequences of big hopes, I abstained from any further negotiations with my greedy imagination, and resorted to the habitual watch of the evening sun falling down the heights of its own enigmatic splendour in untraceable paths, its swollen eye, gently, softly, turn pulpy red before bursting into vivid colours of light and hue - slightly resembling a stabbed bulls-eye. And in that tranquil moment of aesthetic ecstasy did I reflect on human condition, reminisce on childhood in Valliyappanpady, and again and again ponder over what in the name of God I was doing on mother earth, or whatever this floating lake-like reality is supposed to mean; even after countless warnings my disobedient mind slipped into meaningless musings, which most of the times ended in unaided rage and clenching teeth, and just before my unmanageable nerves stiffened rebellious fists in inflated temper, afar, I distinguished with burning eyes the minimised figure of Ibrahim waving hands. On either sides of him were two of his young assistants holding a heavy tripod and his shoulder bag respectively. On top of an excavated cave in half ruins, the members of the archaeological team and documentation crew were sitting meritoriously idle and humming after an intense day of outdoor duties. Done with their work for the day, the crew were about to consume ginger tea and ripened bananas, and I approached the mini-crowd with habitual dialectical confusions. They were all lavish and tender, in contrast to the morning hours of stress and concentration; they discussed the samurai films of Kurosawa, spoke of heavy rains and deadly viruses, and the nearing evolution of my relatively unconventional poetic frame had the small evening talk paused. The earlier assumed air of curiosity in each of their now tired faces seemed vanishing and dissolved away with the going sun. But they put on a new face of intent pleasantness; some appeared plainly comfortable, and as always, our crowd puller boss, apparently unaware of my arrival, went on speaking in high volumes on his political youth, regardless of the general, weary silence. Just below them, inside the dusty cave, men of labour work whispered in monotonous tones about the loud lot above their sweaty heads while impulsively sweeping ancient dust off and away the newly discovered stalagmite floors; one among them, a rather young and fine fellow, made raw fun of the old sweeper beside him who, all throughout his repetitive life, had been doing the often uncredited work of sweeping untidy floors without much recognition or financial benefits. In return, the old worker muttered between his raging teeth, "you too are in line, my young friend," and the small circle of whispering sweepers fell silent, and remained so thereafter, until 18:00 P. M. exhausted dispersions.

In the diminishing red sunset the sailing birds became surprisingly violent and their low flights intense while the tint sky showed gay. Stuck in the endless loop of political conversations and philosophical renderings by those who are totally oblivious to the bitter fact that, in simultaneous collaborations, have exceedingly gone past that age of relevance, my purposeless gaze searchingly penetrated into the interior layers of a slanting, broad tree, whose meditative stillness formed empty spaces of absolute vastness in my mind, and I marvelled over which one was in reality real, the real or the imaginary; and I wondered why, why, why I was destined to think alone, and that I was ultimately living amidst all human suffering, all of human love and hatred and meaningfulness and absurdity in multitudes. I gazed into the depths of motionless trees and again that ridiculous, inescapable adverb spilled into my mind, and in the absolute vacuity stirringly floating through my inner screens, the memory-show began without prior notice, thereby without any active audience but my widowed soul. And I remembered my once masculine hands, full of vigorous energy and overflowing with power and passion, roughly sliding around the pimpled cheeks of my pragmatic wife, then full of life and pride. All is gone, all is lost; I made choices that are irreversible and destructive, and in my defence, no one ever told me the divergent roads ahead led to the same destination.

So here I am, impatiently waiting in silent expressionless exasperation and taking random guesses on whose car will drive me back to my temporary home of white gowns and quiet courtyards, for the school driver had openly displayed reluctance when in the morning was confronted by straight requests for an evening pickup. As a result, like an obedient boy, I furthered my wait in silence for the extended evening to conclusively get over with and the conversing, smiling snack-party to ultimately dissolve into responsible individuals.

Thereby, another low blow to the already sinking energies of my instincts, it was the boss that was picked up at random by the indecisive, clumsy hands of chance to drop me off to the town-school, to its existential backyard outhouse; his nano car sped through the narrow inner shortcuts of the hill-facing villages, splashing mud water from broken water pipes spilled unevenly on the untarred roads. Ibrahim conversing about documentation headaches in the shotgun seat with the indifferent man sunk in the leather steering, I was left alone with the boss' son, whose giant headphones spilled out contemporary electronic beats every now and then. Desperate and longing for love, I gazed out the raised glass and pondered over why cause always preceded effect. Men crossed roads, walked through pavements, drank banana milkshakes or lemon juice in roadside shops, discoursed loudly about business matters or financial dealings, gossiped about other men, but in none of them did I notice themselves; passive men stuck in everyday patterns, unknowingly rolling through existence like a mandatory and default midnight prayer of name-sake relevance, very essential yet burdensome, a secondary prayer involved in getting done with the former, and in absent thoughts that slip away into the horizon of memories like a blurred background, somewhere they will reckon that this life too, was meant to be lived. Somewhere lies theirs and our expecting deathbed, and the transcending revelation is in their understanding that the grand, appalling climax too, like all and nothing, is bracketed within the glassed frames of the transparence in life.

When Ibrahim was dropped off at the footsteps of his cute, two-storeyed and creeper-engaged house, I shifted to the front seat, leaving behind muffled digital sounds, after having shaken firm hands with my old colleague of much memories and gratitude. By the time we reached the green front gates of the catholic primary school, my circulating thoughts were revolving and stuck against the glassed window of the classic building, and a gentle reminder was required to happily let me out the car. The old guard was reciting daily evening prayer, and I very discreetly sneaked in, with the slightest of possible impressions on the ground and delicate, maintained breaths. But a sudden, curious voice paused at once my soundless walk somewhere near to the outhouse courtyard. And somewhere in between conscious steps and thought-filled walks night had imposed itself on the quiet, solitary atmosphere of the hilly town. The fall of night is a free, subtle metaphor, directly proportionate to the discreet, unobtrusive flow of being.

"Mr. Rajan," sounded the voice, charmingly. I turned my sweat-stained head back and saw a tall, healthy figure in a light, ironed *kurta* approaching in steady motion. "Father Abe!" I uttered in deep reverence and some surprise. It was Father Abraham, the Director of the primary school. Few dangling white papers flexed in the cool midnight breeze as his masculine palms gripped them firm under their flapping liveliness. We were standing in the dark in a one-to-one correspondence posture right at the middle of the tiled portion that divided or linked the outhouse to the school building or the other way round. We were standing in the dark and it was not so late but the late-night birds were already crying and the air and its corresponding mood was optimistic and pleasant.

"You look exhausted, Das," remarked the middle-aged priest, rather excitedly, having formally traced and analysed the harshness of the day in my agitated attires. "Come with me to the shades. Here. Yeah, just under the bulb light. Perfect. I wrote a philosophical essay on the pitiful life of dragon flies just today afternoon. It is titled, "What we shouldn't do to Dragon Flies." I want to read it out for you..," after having moved me to a bulb-lit area by the outhouse walls as though I was some controlled fly in experimentation mode, his excited talk got interrupted naturally by the launching of the flappy papers. The wind was blowing overhead, parallel and straight, interrupted, broken and unceasing, signifying existence.

And for ten minutes straight I was exposed to the dire living conditions of these poor fluttering beings called dragon flies whose highly athletic and high-speed standards of life was both hallucinatory and trippy in curious observations.

"Poor, lovely creatures who seek nothing but friendly, humanely affections and care. In return they reserve nothing but high disregard and neglect, for their exceptional abilities and energy shall in this life stand unappreciated. Oh, those, poor poor dragon flies, so glorious their flight is, so vibrant their majestic postures... blessed are their specific attributes, full of charge and variations..."

The back of my body was hurting and the accumulated stuffed sweat of the day turned itchy to the point of complete inattentiveness. All I wanted was a refreshing bathe and a neat sleep. Only if this poor, innocent dragon-fly sympathiser would ever understand.

"... and no man has ever laid his hand upon these colourful insects for no reasons other than pure arrogance!" the oral rendering of the short article came to an aggressive, teeth-clenching finale, and a moment of suspended silence of unforeseeable character followed as my overworked eyes aimed at the simple elegance in front of me in awe. We stood in the dark filled with quietness and reflections, deeply moved and absorbed in the prolonged, magnifying radius of the emotional vibe created by the sorrowful recital that marked its impressions the way a slow-burn western spaghetti film would do. Perhaps it may not have been the depressing nature of the subject, rather the intensity of the emotions evoked that brought our contrasting temperaments to a combined halt of stillness measurable only by compassionate trance.

"Did you have dinner, Das," the father asked me, tenderly, in a very low voice, totally in contrast with the philosophy uttered a few moments ago. Yet something in the air persistently suggested the irrevocable feelings introduced were here to stay.

"No, Father. I had a very long and heavy day and I am extremely tired. I need to take a good bathe now," I responded in humble tones, feeling the deep exasperation accumulating somewhere in me.

"Oh, please proceed then. It is already late. The ladies have left for home early today. They won't be here to provide you dinner. Don't go out now for food. Come down and dine with me after you freshen up. I too haven't had dinner; the seminary cook is preparing fried rice and chicken roast. We can talk more on dragon flies and life in general at the dining table. I'll be pleased to host you tonight," the spiritually attuned symmetrically-perfected confluence spoke with compassion and generosity. It was getting late and more and more tiring and the night was elaborated, so was the cracked tiles in the outhouse front-yard.

*

There was so much tension on the mural Italian painting on the wooden wall of the miniature dining hall solely made use of on lonesome dinners or such small-scale and unplanned occasions. Fleshy, coldblooded meat and rice was served as promised. Well, literally, I had to go and serve it for myself since it was a buffet arrangement and my gluttonous aspirations were followed by the moderated diet of the father that included the fresh, garden-picked likes of berries and grapes and we gladly had our dinner by the radiance of the three pillar-like slender-looking candles located right at the middle of the table and the warmth of the soundless night. The father's running mind got pre-occupied in a series of affairs that directly concerned the school administration and management and most of the time his eyes and its other-half of perceptions was trapped in the brilliant radiance of a mysterious, handy monolith at hand – commonly, collectively, referred to as a smartphone, whose structural evolution and the world of digital fluidity and order - a parallel universe of it own, was in itself a story to tell. Dragon flies and lectures on life had to wait. Electricity repetitively wavered, went on and then off and on again and an off here and an on there, sort of imitating the peculiar charisma of an uncertain youth and my mind – attuned to the determined nature of psychedelic electricity, kept fluctuating between enjoying the fleshy, spicy food in front and the more intriguing painting up above hanging on the walls.

Talkative, whispering classic people murmured and gestured among themselves within their concentrated sub-groups, while a tall, enigmatic figure in glorious attires, with his steady, long hands kept firmly on the wide dining table, appealed to be indifferent and transcending. A lot of hand gestures and draperies was involved and there definitely was a certain, indefinable tension or conspiracy looming in the immediate air. An ocean of symbols and clustered, suffocative leg movements as though innumerable automobiles got stuck in an eternal loop of strawberry-flavoured traffic jam in the whirling highways of Diary Circle, as the hills beyond unaffectedly reposed to the in-build calmness of their greenish, picturesque fluidity, gracefully echoing the ceaseless ecstasy of the person in the middle. Are those roasted meat or boiled, unshaved potatoes? And look, then there's a sharp, shiny knife introduced from out of nowhere. A curved, innocent-looking road leads to the ancient town and the hills beyond. Sharp, deceptive and cunning eyes everywhere. Half-filled glasses of red wine on the table. Aldous Huxley is true, there is something really intriguing about draperies and many a great artists and painters have helplessly tripped on the mysterious intellectual allurement they arouse. Dinner was done with; the crowd dispersed in clever, deceitful whispers and I cleared the emptied plate and washed them clean and bacteria-free, out of decency, before dreamily proceeding to the Sartrean outhouse. There is definitely something captivating about those colour-schemed draperies and about these trippy, sloppy tiles in rosy and bluish tendencies. I am running late, time is giving the impression of recklessness and over-speed. It is Friday night. The fortunate ones will get drunk night and the rest impatiently waits for their turn that is the succeeding day.

Early in the morning of two days past, as I was interpreting the above-described weary night onto bright, digitalised platforms in the comforts of a pleasant view from the creeper-covered, sunbeam-spilled balcony, the extra-loyal guard came pacing noisily through the curved, spoiled staircase that led to the tiled outdoor balcony to inform me of last night's unattended front door, and with tiresome, drained-out eyes warned me of wild, opportunistic dogs seeking for unattended chance - thrown opportunities at unlocked doors so as to find warmth and comfort and pursue a deep, soundless sleep in roofed balconies when the night gets too deep and cold and unbearable. I nodded my head in indifferent agreement; my stirring heart too swayed slightly in pity and in partial dissent and later in complete acceptance of carelessness. In the jelly-like nucleus of these slight movements, I realised in self-contempt that in fact I was the real egoistic. Overhead, where the slanting big trees bearing greenish coconuts or ripened mangoes crossed each other in paths and in motives as part of their ambitious expansion projects, a minute gap opened up to the soothing view of overcast skies in which local birds, after a heavy night's run, roamed aimlessly, very freely, in restful leisure; they could have humbly come down to our fragile earth to fulfil their deserving idleness; they too, like me, are evading reality, either consciously or out of boredom. Drifter, 70's-inspired birds in grey skies, a sea of fallen leaves in soaked grounds, a lot of wrecked ships under blue, algae-licked waters, and then there is a bit of me too. No migraine is to come of today. In a while the official school driver will come to pick me and the journey would be begin, yet another one - a relatively time-draining one: Nilgiris is not more than five hours from here. And I hope the long, hurried road journey would turn out to be a pleasant and enriching one too in terms of images and imageries and that the sidewalks and foggy views are filled with wild flowers and women. Nilgiris is where the mystical and awe-inspiring highly saturated shrubs of *Strobilanthes kunthiana or Kurinji*blooms in 12 years and it is were Prasad Chaithanya, a relatively unknown sage, has his abode - where he pursues his life-long dedication to wisdom and seclusion. Around five-hour long trip is Nilgiris from here but the return journey might take either an eternity or an overnight bus ride. Anyhow, I'll be off in not more than thirty minutes. Luggage is packed. The trippy-looking candle holder lifelessly submitted to heavy winds the other night and lies in mourning on the rain-spilled floors. My wife had gifted the bluish ceramic beauty to me after returning from a family trip to the Kolkata. She is a lovely and sensible person. One stuff leads to another memory and imagination takes advantage of the whole, reverse-gear situation to add a bit of creative topping in the form of extended thoughts on top of the creamed cake. The porcelain holder fell to the floor and broke. It was a favourite and close to my heart but I am an insensitive and cold one. Nilgiris is around 160 kilometres from here. I got an e-pass ready. The officials might ask for one in the border. Free roams are limited and monitored these days. Face masks alone won't do. The old sage lives in an isolated ashram, as far as my restless curiosity was able to dig up. The driver will be here any minute. Luggage has been packed. But the porcelain is on the floor, broken and distorted and unusable. Things, they break, one way or another. When will the driver come? This chapter needs to get done with.

A young priest, tall and handsome, who was residing downstairs - yes, amusing to my own presumptions, I was in fact sharing the outhouse building with another person, happen to pack his bags almost in sync with the Einsteinium relative motion of mine and prepared his leave before the last paragraph was declared completed. His mind was still not steady and tuned to take up responsibilities, I happened to decode later. He has placed his final, existential hopes on a railway exam. The driver will be here any moment and I take a last-minute walk through the backyard and surprisingly encounter tapioca fields beyond the wild, enveloping vegetation. For a moment I believed the accidentally discovered fields to be a phenomenon, perhaps a conspiracy or even a wild guess. Wherever I go, I finally end up in tapioca fields, fresh and still and soft.

CHAPTER THREE

ABOVE SETTLEMENTS

With the Vedantic teachings and philosophical vibes and handed-down wisdom, for the first time in a while my superimposing ego felt dizzy and discomposed and unwillingly lowered itself to cold, freezing zones, leafing around among fellow men of suppressed egos or forgotten selves, but never to dissolving heights. Not yet.

The days piled up in mashed succession from the real-time perspective of a reflective present and my soles bled in constant exposure to branded shoes and persistent coldness intensified by winter and storms and it was November. Amongst the grand splendour of glowing grasses, pure red appealed wicked. Above flourishing settlements, the panoramic, warming view makes any great fool feel important.

Yet I shockingly prefer to remain a mortal idiot in my earthly understandings, for only they yearn for solitude and misty evenings; the vulgar craving for red meat, or any goddamn juicy flesh, and a deep yearning for morning milk had my uncompromising and celebrated spiritual pride – quite recently derived, whirling around in utter disbelief and self-loath before surrendering dispassionately to the cringey fact that I may perhaps be a bourgeois at heart. Well, once I wanted to be filthy rich. Once.

Most of the time it is seven in the morning or it is never too late. Scanning in retrospection at the days that went by in unbelievable velocity, few glimpses of ecstasy was spotted here and there - spread out on boredom-stained bare grasses or there near the spoiled and forsaken backyard garden of the prayer hall overlooking the vast and splendid neighbouring tea estate or for instance even by the overgrown, uncut vegetation in front of the dull, barely used kitchen building. It is boredom and it is yearned isolation. Both induce a strange feeling of longevity or anxious warmth. It is November and sometimes it is seven in the morning or most often the sun is screaming from right above like an upstairs' landlord, loud and fierce.

Winter birds have arrived. The old sage is wise, friendly and accommodative, universal in outlook and resigned in appearance. The day is blonde at seven in the morning and the overlooking hills golden and baked and wise while the crammed room will be cold, stuffy and reflected. The alarm usually goes off right after sunrise. Not always. It may vary though. The sun has bitter mood swings. That does in any way affect or alter the prayer hour: it is fixed and default and unchanged. The prayer is scheduled at nine in the morning and that is uncompromising. And the sage has assigned me with the task of lighting the holy lamp before the commencement of prayer sessions each morning and that is to be maintained and unaltered. Above hilly settlements, it is textbook and old school, and the views are terrific and authoritative.

Mainstream beaches are best for the unmarried novelists; hilltop huts for solid brain-users, and perched on the huge vastness of this secluded grassland like an afternoon bird of melodious idleness, overlooking the colourful colony settlements stretching below, I discreetly pray to myself that I too shall once and for all be allowed to pursue this sometimes boring yet dynamic philosophical life in full, aggressive magnitudes. Somewhere in me is a transparent wall that needs immediate levelling, but ridiculously impossible to penetrate through with pointed thoughts; weak and soft, yet so unbreakable and impenetrable; through the see-through, emotionless bricks I seek with a mouth wide open and a throbbing heart *that* mysterious thing or nothing lurking behind in eternal fashions. Sadly, some vague fog prevents my burning gaze from advancing further, halting its infinite motion right at the onset of the divine blurriness. What is it? I do not have clear answers. Why is it in me? ... It is getting late once again, I need to get back to my new transcendental shed, for I fear terrestrial creatures, and all philosophical interactive sessions have been postponed to an unannounced date somewhere in the near future. For it is getting dark outside, the storms are breaking in the distant, bluish skies in roars and in lightning flashes. It is winter; legs are cracked and dry, brownish and dirty. The days are fierce and trembling, the rains have come. Imagination lurks around abandoned corners and dampened grass, vague and carried-away, indistinct and slippery. What time is it, I cannot recall.

The collapsing sun in its subdued glory threw muted gleams of faint lights, turning pale gold the upper portion of the vast, mostly uncultivated stretch of curved hills beyond the glassed hut I am currently inhabiting as an unofficial caretaker or an unknown poet in desperate search of mad inspiration; whatever you may like to term my meaningless follies. In a matter of floating moments, night is to close in on this splendid view of the semi-colonised misty hills that is the only source of some motivation for my early-morning, sleep-induced consciousness to stretch and expand; the thick pine forests under the pale hills, where historic, small-scale communities live in pure harmony and seclusion, have gone untouched in the divine rays of the diminishing sun. Wild dogs bark fiercely outside the glassed doors in savage and unison harmonies; they badly want me out for a brutal encounter, but them poor creatures cannot digest in any way the utter fear of the pathetic coward these semi-bricked walls are containing in total absence of activity or reason. It is time for the electronic spiritual bells to resonate, awakening the sleepy hill-town, who are always passive and inattentive to their own virtual callings. Soon the gloomy settlement will shine softly under the subtle glory of bulb lights and loud speakers streaming selected verses from Holy Scriptures. Loud rickshaws and automobiles are draggingly wheeling their way through the curved roads leading to their uphill homes; their working day has ended in modest profits; mine is still lurking behind endless gazes and existential reveries. I check my WhatsApp installation now and then just for some unexpected, fallen visits. Nothing. Nobody. No one.

Time must have floated like soothing waves in the background, for the ready-made dawn has already broken beyond the blurry windows and the sleepy hills; my trembling hands, muffled in Halloween gloves, struck vigorously another hardened match stick - this time giving birth to a relatively small yet intense flame, its enigma reflected on the blurry glass in front in faint descriptions; last night's heavy storm has its remains in wet forms glued on every barred glass in front of me. Baskin' Robbins-patented skies transitioned and mystified: a new day is silently forming in the background. I stay still and prepare myself to not to be carried away by the cold breeze or colder imagination, not to shudder in this undisturbed solitude, but remain ethical to the eternal vows I once promised to whoever it may concern. Under erotic flames I warm my soft and tender heart; the intense smell of burned wool still clinks on this yawning air even after continual exposure to the morning breezes, and I feel old and done, but I know with utmost clarity that the suppressed youth in me, like a crouching tiger in hiding, is patiently waiting for the exact moment to show up in some vintage style.

Damn.

Above awakening settlements, sun rises carefully, understandingly. Yet delicate, yellowish beams were spilled around carelessly, awakening the quiet, drowsy dreams of a withdrawn expanse: after a drowsy night of small talks and television pass-times, civilisation has finally risen and is back on refreshed legs and unchanged tracks. In a moment happy cries of playful kids and foggy lights of farmer trucks will bring the valley-settlement back to normal hours, and remains of last night's boiled rice still awaits me in the Chinese cooker, but I, with resigned eyes and a frozen soul, reflect for more than an unnoticeable hour it must have been now, on the inevitable and irreducible aspects of daily life. From down below, women of the cauliflower fields are heard yelling native curse words: some knocked-out man must has misbehaved in the morning.

Usual, terrible scenes.

Near to the narrow, overgrown pathway that leads to the vast layers of grass growing on the raised grounds of my yesterday's half-sleeps and half-dreams, two soft, yellow butterflies are spotted fluttering away in mild speed, while far away on the hard hills wrapped in fog and cloud, some white birds with elongated peaks, resembling plain sailor boats, so passively and adorably fly across the thick union of pine trees comprising the evergreen forest; I do not understand the philosophy of birds, they glide around so freely as though they are some exceptional and exempted souls preferentially freed of the complaining ego's daily doses; I should admit I utterly envy their carefree and downright lives. They are free to fly, to be perpetually lost, the divine skies are theirs; for all I know of all the mere information I've gathered so far, man is eternally lost - at least ontologically.

Transcendental ontology.

Crackling sounds of splitting firecrackers unreflectively change my sunk gaze from the bright touchscreens in hand to the bulb-lit becoming settlements of Fern hill; sloping slightly irregular, forming almost an inverted curve, and amidst these untimely distractions, carefree reveries, inescapable burdens of daily life, appalling reflections on existence, cool nights of upcoming winter, I often tend to forget to reflect on the absurd reality that I too exist somewhere in between these floating formalities.

All the rusty mirrors blackened, all muddy waters turned obscure, and all the shattered glasses transitioned foggy and indistinct, the overcast images of my decay got lost in the divine impotencies of my own burning eyes. Hazy smokes leaking from heavy breathing, my current time-moving activity, illuminated only by the pointed flame, mingled smoothly with the faint fumes emitted from the burning candle, and in the blurred backgrounds, the dim blue skies reveal gay shades of tinge, announcing the grand gradual entry of the golden sun in all its mystical magnificence, while in its blissful discernments, these unfortunate words spill out of my moist mouth prior to my own personal understanding of the same: "Yet another day. Nothing is to come of it."

And I dejectedly sit, perched in the depths of moving imaginations and silent gazes, having my morning cup of warm water and breathing out visible smokes. This ever flowing time seems such an absurdity because there is nothing to contrast it with, like night for day, or tea for coffee. Only if somehow I could effortlessly manage to override this inescapable existence and chill with eternity in the promised lands.

Ha.

For how long have I been soberly tripping on this cracking dawn and the transitioning hills?

Someone knocked at the closed doors, and fully awakening from my half-endorsed and warmed consciousness, I hastily rush to the front hallway, my hurried movements almost tripping on the wet mats of morning's spilled ecstasies, only to be confronted by the bohemian image a lone and worn drifter awaiting me in classic coolness outside, ahead of the melancholic and overgrown lawns in front. His eyes were swollen of heat and time, few clouds of grey hair stood out of the rather unkempt and savage-like, long beard, and dark patches of dry hair sprayed around the chestular, unbuttoned area and he remained calm and cool as though he was forever entitled to be so; he was wearing a classic Pepe Jeans' shirt, torn and faded and evergreen, of light-brownish cheques, and he stood there all right, gazing straight into the eyes with an elated smile, something sort of like I was the second man on earth.

"Hello... uhm..," he spoke softly but firmly, searching for words. "I was an inmate of this community twenty years ago, just like you're now. It was during Yeti's times; it is all very different now; only that little cottage and this mahogany tree is preserved from then. Back in those days the whole place was occupied by hippies, artistes and intellectuals and it was flourishing. Well, what shall I call you? A sage?" he asked, politely.

And I was immediately struck with an inner battle. "What should I be called," I opened out to myself, confused and bewildered.

I struggled for words, he sensed it immediately, and wisely dealt with it.

"Yeti and I were really close; I used to accompany him in most of his interstate trips on rails. But I haven't been around for a very long time. I heard through former friends of his unfortunate demise. But by then I had gone too far away..." these words he spoke in English, turning his half-lost gaze to the vibrant blue skies above.

"Chaithanya Prasad resides here now; he takes care of the place now. In the extreme end of the upslope in front, in between the union of pine trees, is his hut," I said, pointing my directions to the raised slopes to the right where thick, spread-out plants stood still and erect, barring the gestured directions midway.

"Is it? Well, that will do away with the current confusion. He will recognise me for sure. See you," he said this in restless tones of sudden hope, and wasting no time, proceeded uphill through the scorching stone-steps before covering his bearded face with a crimson towel.

Shortly afterwards, while mildly contemplating on my disrupted appetite and pondering over which of the limited varieties of dry biscuits to have from the stocked packets for my purposefully delayed lunch, a rather puzzled woman by my open doorsteps introduced herself in the native language as the unofficial maid, and began explaining solemnly about the old sage's precise instructions to take care of my grocery needs during the fifteen day quarantine period (twelve or more of which has already gone by). Her fragile lungs, she spoke in utmost seriousness and pain, was severely affected by the storms of November. Her stunted hut in the basement-level valley below the plantations was under the government radar in suspicion for slightly spilling over a couple of metres or more over a private property whose owner is in serious talks with the local authorities for the conception of a prime resort, and, thereby, in order to meet the collector and fight for her ancestral land, she took a hurried leave, earnestly promising to come back the very next day that went on forever or more.

Thereafter she soaked-up my dried-up vegetable container in a handful of fresh vegetables, a can of salt and cooking oil and a glass bowl of brown rice, and for the first time in a while that may have exceeded a lifetime, raw vegetables cooked in minimal levels and boiled rice sprinkled over it and later fried together appealed to be a heavenly discourse shadowily interpreted to ontological flows.

Blue, broken skies turn pale in streamlined sets of clouds of refined violet, resembling precisely with the tensed yet most adorable skies of Da Caravaggio's unbelievable painting I am now curiously spying on with appalling empathy, for I totally fear this infinite resignation; now and again I tell you, I reemphasise, that my sole motivation to be here in wilderness of aloneness is to escape the endless gazes of passive men and not merely for highly scholarly intercourses. Yet in my darkest hours of revolving curiosity I betray my own dreadful fear and probe into the undecipherable absurdities; only if life had been a little less self-contradictory. The grand sun has taken its leave in dissolving hues, and in a detached state of mind I light the conifer-like candle lying on the closed windowsill, but when I burn the narrow dust-filled ledge with a flaming matchstick, my conclusive mind spots no melting wax, and I, for a moment, fell short of ready-made answers; the burning candle laughed hysterically at my lack of general intelligence, and I too for my part helplessly mocked at my undernourished instincts.

The bearded drifter drinking lavishly in a local pub or a dance bar with the few blessed rupees Chaitanya Prasad had spared, and afterwards hitting the road again; the old maid preparing dinner as she gazes out with justifiable rage, the clouding tears in her eyes blur the protected green land beyond the bamboo fence of her elegant backyard, and in introspection, or in a re-enactment of a particular scene in memory from the other angle, I indirectly enter the strange consciousness of that peculiar old sage of this totally isolated compound, who, in his undefined stroll through the late evening dried grounds, sees the faint, candlelit features of my grumpy face, and through the momentary and short-lived startlement that instantaneously faded away to massive indifference, I saw with secondary eyes the dim and gloomy image of my own candlelight emptiness. Another night has fallen. Even the distant stars in the dark skies and the cracked moon have completely disappeared. It is all very empty. If I was the first man I would've grasped different subtle moon for each varying night. I wish I was one; I would for ever trade these factual earthly certitudes for eternal blurriness.

Through dry and overgrown paths I quietly walk in calm rebellion against the winds, existence and migraines; under bright blue skies of heavenly elegance I spit on those tender and loveable glowing daffodils of great passion by the untamed gardens, turning pale and gloomy their natural splendour under the influence of my pure and transparent waters, and on my way back, without a simple deviation or double thoughts through the same old half-savage green, I tried to convince my trained mind that this evergreen reality is nothing but stored images. Then it stormed on Fern hill and heavy, vibrating thunders reigned all over the isolated existence of this spiritualist high terrain, and it stormed continuously for almost a week or more. When all the great roars and lightning finally receded and pawed way for a clear hue sky, the digital alarm sounded a bit too late than usual, I suspect, for staring in half-asleep mode into the depths of the white bulb-light reflection splattered on the pinkish tiles mingled with an agitated bush of pipe water spilled over the toilet floor surface, a deep-felt doubt over the authenticity of the recorded rendering of the British soft rock song heard faintly from my room across the dark hall engulfed my awakening consciousness; what surety do I have to blindly confirm it with a reality status? Is not this faint resonance happening in my lazy head? For that also is inaccurate; since my head too is on the outside, part of the external? Is it not then the reality that I am at this moment just a mere representation of an endless void, from whose omniscient clutches some ethereal substance badly wanted an escape, thereby running away in its own reduced might to thoughtlessly float in this damned reality which is nothing but its own private cave of momentary escape?

When mixed with cold milk and packeted oats, native banana attains a seemingly high and other-worldly status; good food satisfies your cravings, while green food pleases the transcendental aspects. So did I have my sophisticated Monday breakfast, while gloomy birds of the Western Ghats crowded around my glassed exterior windowsill, some resting serenely by the pale green grass where my colourful boxers coldly waits for some more thrown sunshine overriding through the over-imposing authority of the hills. Soon the faint sound of sickle slashing hard grass evade through my absent morning ears, and I hurriedly run down the narrow pathway to the evergreen grass-grounds below with my old Nikon D5300 hanging by my shoulders in suppressed excitement, for the moment to shine has come again after a very long time of suffocated idleness; black dogs of fierce teeth and terrifying growls representing grave demonic aggression chase me down the widespread greens, unheeding to the vain shouts of the old mower - their only master, and to my panic-stricken, horror-filled yells. Tired and trembling, I lock up my damnation room in aggravating anxiety, taking a deep vow to not to return to that enormously vast and incomprehensible existential wall that is the outside world, until the dates for the day of final revelations has been officially declared.

So I sit here all day like a melted-down wax candle on this wooden and broken, paint-reined chair of a bygone artist's last struggle, motionlessly waiting in mild angst for post-winter rains to come and soften these *Maya*-blue wax of early morning soul hunting and undisturbed desolation. This is my untamed life of soft temptations and great regrets. This is my silent riot, my eternal indifference.

My sensitive palms crack in pale intersections, revealing clogged blood; they paint my glassed windows black, and they pelt stones at the drunk drifter. Then they will come back again to knock with their bended sticks at my freedom doors. But I'll be long gone then, floating in calm, mystical oceans.

An ambitious man. A man submerged and driven by his own take on reality.

An unconventional, avant-garde version.

Then the heavy winds straight outta the Arabian oceans blew, revitalising the settlements, and with them arrived the harsh overseas rains; tiled rooftops kept crackling in the unstoppable rains of the indestructible night, and the sliced moon softened and smudged in the heaviness of the skies like a water-coloured sketch. Melodiously, artistically, it melted in the darkened, mystified skies. In the heart of the fierce, domestic rivalry between elements of nature, immigrant birds temporarily conquered the untamed front courtyard, and waking up a bit late than usual, I felt the firm earth below trembling, for the crystal green hills, after the eventual fall of the dense floating morning fog, now sublimely glorified in the becoming sun: it too occurred to be quavering. It was seven in the morning once again. In deep-sleep mode hours, twisted and curved and warped, smashing against one another's compressed mixture similar to the squashed mentality of a mixed fruit jelly-like preparation. It was seven in the morning. Midnight dreams followed imagination's will.

Seven in the morning.

Seven thirty in the head.

Delayed distortion.

07.07 AM.

Snapshots of thoughts that resemble swarms of bees.

Thoughts of seven in the morning.

Thoughts of blue in clogged waters.

And the heavens open their omniscient gates for a short, calculated six minutes in the wake of a sustained, timely progression of tremendous progressive soft rock outflow. That unparalleled, comfortable solo resonates freely in my melancholy room as I myself existentially overflow in eternal bliss. During that brief moment of pure ecstasy, like a freed balloon gasping for breath in the air, I ambiguously wander around the transcendental lyrics like a comfortably confused teenager, as though "lost in thought and lost in time."

And the solo erupts, divine and meditative and blissful, sending charged tremors up and down the numbed soul.

Floating winds sweep the silvery skies clean. In the aftermaths of the abrupt clearing the mystical hills reveal its cosmic splendour. Heavenly foams, white and thick and creamy, drip fluidly down the smooth salient curves: the southern hills of crystal green features, with all its spiritual glories, too, were met with a mild orgasm, inevitable and calming.

In the intense, intellectual winters of the Nilgiris, palms crack and reveal maps of unknown, symbolic oceans and continents - palms that are pinkish and dried, fleshy and cracked, maps of transcendental geography and oceans of inexplicable configurations.

CHAPTER FOUR

THE SOLITARY SAGE

One vignette morning in the month of merry celebrations, when stimulating hills semi-consciously hid behind thick swamps of flooding mists, the old, pony-tailed and white-bearded sage woke from soft dreams and visions and in a meditative mood loosely surrendered again his common wakeful state to deep-sleep. After a short recital of a customary Upanishadic chant, the old sage, with his lone new student by the crimson mat evenly spread on the cold floor, commenced the morning class sessions with a thorough lecture on pure consciousness smoothly oscillating, like fluttering bees, through its own four-fold schematic structure, unbelievable and wonderful, mysterious and all-encompassing; effortlessly he drove the ever-moving tyres of wisdom from one subject interest to another, like croaking frogs skipping slippery stones all the way down to rippling rivers. From deep mystical oceans to modern opulent economics when the rag and rough leather stick shifted gears in rapid procession, there was total silence thereafter, for the wise man was equipped with no spoken words thereafter, and the amateur disciple lagged way behind in thoughtfully striven attempts at comprehension; the morning session ended with another holy rendering, and both of us had a modest brunch by the untamed lawns overlooking the rising settlements where he attentively ate bananas and spoke of his disastrous personal life and of his bohemian youth.

"It was back in the immortal, indestructible 70's, the golden era of free rides and savage love. We got along very well and became close friends too. Then one day we went for a long walk through the valley down the tea estates. Next morning she abruptly packed her bags and took the first train back to her hometown. I didn't hear from her for the next couple of months but by the end of autumn floods of postal letters amplifying rage and frustration wrapped up my being. Thankfully, by the coming of winter things gradually settled down and our relationship found a normal course. The postmen at both ends of the irresistibly desirous postal connection witnessed a virtual spark or a glow. The signed letters slowly started getting stacked up in each of our respective study tables, and soon the country post offices became a sheer necessity. Months and years and worms and everything in this stacked-up, contained ontology went by, and got along well with one another's mysterious absurdity. And one fine day the warmness and comfort these sealed covers I received contained transformed itself tremblingly into faint, appalling scribbles written in stained crimson and not ink blue; and they stung of life, pure and irresistible..." he reminisced, his swollen eyes still gleaming in horrifying memories and relative time got mashed and mixed up in free, transferrable emotions in the likes of an elitist potato for a sophisticated dinner.

In the evening the sage of reminiscences and good memories gave life lectures in mild and lowered tones, in the depths of which a devoted disciple was to sink for complete understanding and fruitful results. With invisible twinkling beads revolving around his clasped hands in nice, rhythmic motion, he meditatively circled both his wrinkled thumps against one another like the earth meditatively trailing around the sun, during the whole of the chanting of concluding devotional prayers. "Life on earth is paradoxical," concluded him with deep and retired eyes.

Harmless cows embrace raised meadows, naive kids of the country throw water bottles on elevated grounds, yet it was the wild wild boars of the valley woods that chased me down the archival rails to those uninhibited sections of the woods that brought back along with the whistling winds, evergreen memories of a lost passion: she was mere human, but my melting soul granted her a divine status. All the heavens and earth mingled in delayed glory at the decaying reminiscence of a former life. I narrowly escape the thick woods, only to witness men of the working class, like half-alive, psyched-out zombies, carrying heavy two sacks of yesterday's big harvest. I return gaspingly to the old man's untold wisdom.

Burning memories in yellow pages; corroded saucepans making distorted grunge noise in the ongoing midst of a hue sunrise. From deep sleeps I emerge a novel man; for I no longer feel the same old adrenaline rush or any cold-blooded urges. Goodbye to youthful, endless aggressions. I am a refined man already, I just can't get up and energetically make use of this wakeful state to any deeper compassions or materialistic fractions. I go to the ponytailed sage, who is silently gazing into the depths of his own oceans, for I can clearly listen to the waters ripple, the waves forming creamy foams in the caramel shores and the seas moving in blissful images. But my absorbing gaze seem incapable to transcend the horizon of error. "*That* which is beyond experience, but at the same time the experience and the experiential - for and of all," spoke he in a greatly contemplative and emotional mood.

The future holds good prospects.

The blind prospects of the future intellectually corresponds to the promiscuous image of an overcooked bowl of Maggie noodles. The many possibilities and chances hang suspended and lie disciplined and stirring in an obscured state of orderly uncertainty and each of the random, unsorted thread-like content of the slippery, bewildered noodles has to be carefully sorted and nicely extracted before the futuristic, modernistic feast begins. Some pale and salty, others golden and rich and glowing, they emerge to the foreground and may instantaneously or accidentally slip down the twinkling spoon like a schoolboy in a playground slide.

By afternoon the flawless reality resigned to its ceaseless flow as usual and my fragile and easily flexible imagination got carried away yet again, in the incoming winds, winters and entanglements of WhatsApp forwards.

And later into the day, in the fog-blurred, mystified outskirts of a cold evening, I consumed strong coffee in the open air. It surely has been over a year or more now since my practical consciousness obediently submitted to the indefinable strength of caffeine overdose. Something in me made stirring noise, and this heavenly feeling of being part of society appealed to me very much. On my way back I slipped on the damp and dirty roads of last night's heavy rains, while a beautiful woman from one of the colourful houses of the settlements below was calling out to her escaped pup in caring tones from the dim and blinded balconies. Though that sublime face never occurred or get hooked in the alert twinkles of my senses for simple grasps, and the miserable fact that I didn't care a bit to turn back and capture that adorable image of her youthful liveliness for eternal storage, I know by the unadulterated gentleness in her soothing, subdued cries the unlimited pleasantness stored within. As I turn from dampened paths past muddled waters, the vintage pocket clock hung swingingly on my right index finger signals to me in humbled suggestions that it is time to sleep. But I need to first get this medieval dirt off my unpolished history. Something only of vague affiliations had hinted to me beforehand about the sweet obstacles waiting calmly for my reappearance inside the fenced philosophical territory, for the great continental cyclone preceded my dragging entrance, and in the mild absence of any natural reflection, my cautious steps encountered one or more slithering creatures rolling their way through the maddened earth, but none dare lay their venomous touch on my trembling subjectiveness; as far as I could reckon, they too must have gone through a delicate crisis at the alarming realisation that this general, shared and rented-out earth might as well collapse all at once at the tragic death of either of their private consciousness.

Perhaps. Unsure.

Maybe.

May-being.

Mayday.

May.

Maya.

Like a spiritless apparition, an enlarged image of cosmic mortality, the bearded sage in his pinkish ragged attires passes by my shivering figure without even an accidental nod of acknowledgment, as though he had turned the indifference mode on with Mother Nature and all its perishable add-ons. Savoy spinach leaves freshly plucked from the mini-sized Monet-inspired hotbed garden bunched tightly in his wet, mud-covered hands, the old sage ascended the slippery steps to his old overgrown cabin on the upslope in anxious indifference to the highly devastative exterior conditions, as if - as a result of the timeless wisdom accumulated throughout the years, the uphill federations had willingly granted him some sort of a vague preference or a relief, or even an affectionate exception. His deep, desolate eyes glowed in the faint torchlight and his introverted face reflected unimaginable depths, psychic, cosmic or incomprehensibly indefinite.

My glassed room was stinging of rotten banana peels, and I locked it from the inside, double-checked it in hereditary compulsions, and went to bed in slight envy to the solitary sage's remarkable capacity for a complete unresponsiveness that was totally convincing and sound and understandable and inspiring.

Detached. A split. Reason? Alone.

It is not just caffeine that is drawing my memory-driven imagination closer to the open snack shop by the woods. Rather I prefer to wholeheartedly accept and recognise life as a wholesale deal, a comprehensible obscurity: the totality of the whole experience of drinking coffee by the open shop in the woods - involving naughty winds and unexpected rains, is what stirs my restless mind, and instils an inspiration of a deep craving for more and more.

Caffeine.

On a side note, Nilgiris is full of wild flowers and horses.

Like hot steams uninterruptedly rising from fuming bath tubs, thick clouds of morning mist form their own exclusive layered designs in between the broad pines and mystical hills; only then, only then did it occur to my logical confirmations that the forests and the hills and all that is existentially unavailable to me, did not altogether exist as one or a single layer. Rather, each of the distinguishable, respectable entities were secured with their own personal spatial validity. Yet, all through these days of absent gazes and later retrospections, in the grim absence of any dividing mists, each and everything undoubtedly occurred to the senses to be an integrated dish.

At this very integral moment of cross-intersection between I don't know what and which, let me take a brief break from meaningless drifts through the *samsara* to reorganise myself with the subject matter at hand, that is either our old contemplative or indifference.

A couple or more days it must have been since I last attended these side notes from my mostly unattended being. Either I don't get time or there is too much of it, rich and overloaded like leaking hot chocolate and some days' time is obscured, suspended or screeched. The past couple of days were wrapped and concealed under the rein of a tremendous, unbearable migraine spell. My peaceful sleeping hours have been affected unconditionally by the sudden changes in weather - both spatial and inextensive, I assume so, for surreal, incomprehensible dreams and those that defy regular laws seem to fully engage my slippery consciousness during cold nights.

One thick moody morning that is today, when the heavy fogs engulfed even the big mahogany tree in the front courtyard of our creeper-invaded prayer hall, Chaitanya Prasad walked down the twinkling footpaths of slender grasses with his usual contemplative inwardness of mind, matter and awareness and a silvery hot-water bottle, as I automatically threw the fresh carrot head I was holding onto like a thoughtless onlooker to the short shrubs in front, in previously implanted instincts of raising wild roots, and perhaps by the magical grace of some powerful superior entity.

"The maid didn't turn up today," I informed the old master in a very casual voice, trying to sound cool and free. We were standing facing one another by the extended kitchen premises below.

"Yeah, in these harsh weathers she often takes leave. Her house is deep into the valley, and she has to climb all the way up the high slopes of the tea-plantation. It is very risky for her. I suggest you better have some garden vegetables and white rice cooked for yourself for the day," he spoke, conventionally, getting settled within the premises of the kitchen and heading towards the water purifier.

"I had some heated bread with mixed fruit jam. I just said in case you were expecting food..," I remarked, rather puzzled.

"Oh, I stopped expecting things way long back, son," he remarked in a melancholically wise and subdued smile, one that marvellously contained within its subtleties all the highs and lows and crises and laughters of life.

Soon we were talking and walking relaxedly through the wetted grounds back to the prayer house up ahead. Through the misty morning we ambled, me following him, and I discreetly captured with my silenced Nikon shutter button his white, well-maintained ponytail hanging down the slouchy winter cap, all the while pretending to be eyeing a *Maya* bird perched in meshed branches. Got to be on the safer side, you know. And the day unfolded in front of us, within and without, up and beyond, in well-balanced and novel ways, as it usually does, purely in accordance to Bergsonian standards.

The village is dead silent; only the wild barks of untrained dogs of the valley now and then interrupted the appreciable peace of the cold, hilly atmosphere. Through the blissful scenery of the valley muddy waters ascend down the neighbouring steeps, and in no time the overflowing canals announce the coming of the north eastern rains.

To move along with the eccentric thrills of a mad, horizontalised world in itself is a dangerous business; a dark cloud of thousand eyes seem to always follow you, revolve around you like a hive of concentrated bees; consistently on masked alert, a puff of light smokes there or a yellow magazine somewhere is all it takes for the eyes to then turn cold and cringed and suspicious, and the public opinion and commonly acceptable levels to degrade instantaneously and fall drastically.

After three long days of maintained, disciplined rains and intense fogs, the awaited sun revealed itself above the hills in its underexposed and celebrated pride. For throughout history its exhaustive and unimaginably immense energy has been exposed, observed, analysed, scrutinised, interpreted, translated, researched, symbolised, idolised and ultimately, acknowledged and revered, to a certain extent, even feared and thereby hailed and worshipped too.

I keep wandering through the escalating, updated social media profiles of my old college-mates and peers as though I was once and for all slipped and merged into the lifeless consciousness or power driving a pale, disconnected autumnal leaf down the plantations in the irregular, chaotic spell of the winds. Astonishingly, the rest of the autumnal yellowish characters were doing pretty good and were well-off with regular incomes and decent Saturday-night parties and every slight curve ascend through the hierarchical, crowded career ladders turn envious and monitored in times of tight hours and competitive affairs.

Half-native, half-imported towns flourishing on tourism, souvenirs, honeymoon fantasies and recreated traditions make one feel life on earth is an accidental slip; some cosmic punk somehow hacked eternal configurations and managed to quietly, unimaginably, override existence, beyond which he lushly entertained himself by stretching singularity like a soft and flexible rubber band. That moment, that very moment of fluid, uncontrollable ecstasy - that which is loosely translated as this, where man half-blindly stages a tragi-comical drama within the boundless walls of a grand theatre, while helplessly confined under the mystical confinements of a stretched elastic.

Lost walks carry along with its pleasant and exhaustive characteristics some highly creative energy that appeals to be completely foreign and translated from elsewhere; and this mysterious tendency of mine echoes indie vibes on beautiful landscapes and rose gardens or highways while the solitary sage's, I presume speculatively, on baking breads, jeep rides and Sunday pancakes.

Judgements.

An abrupt and complete stoppage of this aggressive, irreverent reality is a matter of high concern for Chaithanya Prasad, for in casual speeches passing anxiety is incidentally evoked in tremendous fright. It is the case with most of the white-haired man or woman of this brutally overused earth. When news of a novel virus poured out last winter in ravaging speed, I remember myself walking down the dusty highways of Andhra Pradesh in inexplainable dread. I can only imagine what it'll be like for those up ahead in the yearly scale.

But a man of wisdom reckons very well that death is only a posteriori hypothesis, for man knows death only by mourning to his dear ones, and never ever to his own; one must be placed beyond being to fully realise death in its proper experiential sense, and no else could've mastered such transcendental experiments than the retired hippie himself. But, yeah, everyman loses his temper and footholds once thrown excessively to the rustic entanglements of sensational and news-worthy episodes of the day.

Perhaps there is a common denominator running down the aisle of life.

Sudden winds showered piles of glared, overexposed soft leaves, and only then did the drowsy senses took into consideration the sun-bleached tree swaying mutely beyond the blazing grasses, for, till then, I was drowned immensely in an imaginarily recreated passionate room with my childhood sweetheart. An unreflective compromise was always necessary. And they say time is remembered in spatial points; they don't reckon that it can be gently evoked in clinging ideas or lovely scents of bohemian strawberries freely available from realms of imagination. But unlike stuffy rooms overwhelmed in the arousing flavours of strawberry condoms, sunburnt trees from the world of *samsara* do not seem to be fuelled up by freewill; mind needs to feed it regularly with liberal thoughts of no ends.

For the past many inactivated years I have been feeding my consciousness with images and effects, embarrassments and regrets. Now I assume this to be the most suitable hour to sprinkle it with some offbeat wisdom streaming from the elderly mouth of an 'unconventional personality, as he once recalled his great master, the grand unifier.

Over the days, with the scorching sun and changing moods, me and the old sage got along surprisingly well, for the crystallised meditative mind seemed to have happily entrusted a slice of his consciousness upon my shrunken existence.

By the end of November, on a fine windy morning in the midst of a sunburnt hour a restless man surrounded by his proud family banged fiercely and continuously at the glassed doors of the closed reception hall building. I was taking a relaxed bath inside. Nothing much happened. He just kept banging on the door unceasingly and I carried on with the warm, geezer-blessed bath, my sense of the world and the moment stuck indefinitely like on an endless loop on the glossy image of the pinkish wall and the broken lines of water spilled over it. The banging never stopped and soon the pinkish image and the sound merciless knocks seemed to get along pretty well like denim shirt and denim trousers of contrasting match.

*

The end of December was approaching, and life amusingly seemed changed altogether; a novel one had formed unknowingly in the obscured or abandoned backgrounds. Christmas was yesterday or day before. Days get mashed and mixed up in the hazy fogs of memories like the pathetic condition of an overcooked *biryani* where both rice and gravy acquire a highly saturated tinge of brownish-ness, finding harmony in the confused, mixed-up melody.

On foreground focus points, I witnessed pasted raindrops helplessly slipping down the glass-panes like an abstract watercolour painting or monotonous waves of rippled waters. On a fine, pleasant morning that was slowly cheering up from the other day's hangover from heavy rains and storms and midnight ecstasies, through the droplets-stuck windows, the world appealed to be squashed and dripping and moist in the artistic likes of an apple-pie pudding or an out-of-focus portrait photograph.

On foreground focus points, I saw another aspect of the highly saturated or graded consciousness in pasted raindrops helplessly slipping down the glass-panes like an abstract watercolour painting or monotonous waves of rippled waters.

The rains once again poured out and relieved themselves.

And the poor leaves shivered pathetically in the cold rains like hopeless fibre knots in the hands of a weaving artisan.

A simple and vital question pervaded time, evades space, and transcends subjective limitations. A simple yet unexplainable one; why are we installed with the power of comprehension?

The bread is baked. Consciousness dissolves, heats itself up, and is salted and oiled, punched and flipped, and ultimately opened up and revealed to rendered bliss.

Multiplied. Reduced. Two-fold. Raised.

So much of bits and pieces of a fallen reality to gather in one gaze.

It is a busy day in town. The infinite roars of the automobile engines has lately assumed the loud impression of an endless alarm of everlasting loop.

The crowded town has collectively abandoned surgical masks; nobody fears, they have happily forgotten that super-microscopic entity which once upon a time few months ago locked them up tremblingly in their homes. The collective ego (which adheres to the likes of myself, of course) has nicely, cunningly, retained the unnecessarily superior feeling of ease and authority, something that is short-lived and careless.

A bored shopkeeper immediately rises from his dull chair to very respectfully welcome a wandering photographer to his shop. Unfortunately, the sight of ancient flies escaping the latter's timeworn wallet discouraged him to the point of raging exhaustion.

In broken roadside mirrors I chance upon the shattered reflection of an old comrade; we seem to recognise each other, but after the split second of standstill glance, we move past each other like highway strangers. All familiar and decodable faces in this animated hill town, except that indifferent reflection.

A middle-aged woman sitting in the lone backseat of an Ola cab gazes out the stuffed window with a melancholic expression on her fatigued face. She is an existentialist. Her thoughts are drifting in revengeful hostility, drowned halfway in impatient waiting for the promised revolution.

Outmoded scarecrows conserve, by ways of fear-mongering in spellbindingly charming and novel fashions, virgin fields.

Once in English literature class I suppose, all were asked to give a small speech on any topic of personal interest, and I, the wannabe cool guy, happened to quote one of Cobain's queer words, leading to much controversy and unpleasant aggression.

Those were the days of unreflected estimations, of inactivated ego; immature and stupid.

With these sticky shameful memories from a gloomy past hanging on my tired shoulders like a pale, fluorescent reflection of the gloomy skies during sunset hours, unable to be disposed casually and faintly traceable, I walk back to the secluded territory, the solitary man's grand affair, in obsessive indifference to life and its backstage mischiefs.

"Where are the hippies?" I shout in roaring determination. "Where have they all vanished?" I pronounce in growing impatience.

"One of them is here, eating boiled potatoes and contemplating in peaceful harmony for eternal bliss," confirmed a calm voice in compost impassiveness. It was the solitary sage. He was dining alone in the broken kitchen hall or elsewhere, psychologically.

CHAPTER FIVE

DAY OF LOST-NESS

Carefully analysing the indefinitely many the dangerous hatreds and dirty ego with painful eyes, sometimes I personally envisage good imaginary spaces and laugh uncontrollably, cracking adorable jokes and forming good brotherhood; in lonesome woods, empty roads, magical towns, cold nights, sweet imaginary outings, adorable reminiscences, and sometimes, in midnight washroom reveries too I remain a solitary passion, a subtle spirit, a wanderlust addict, a gentleman or truly humane.

Chewing grass has become my new pastime activity. It is soothing and very relaxing and savage-like and very medieval and authentic: the historic flavour of raw nature lingering onto my taste buds while I blankly gaze into the depths of a cloudless blue sky and of the splendid grey or dark green prime leaves of an enormously grown unknown tree, each and every minute, easily escapable details in the magnificent abyss of a deeply isolated landscape survived solely by the untouched hands of the greedy high men of society.

People afar chatter loudly out of ignorance, few morning birds render pure harmony for no apparent reason and naked green grass, fresh and twinkling, sparkle shamelessly, revealing even the microscopic outlines and transparency of their slender, tube-like veins. There is a dark cloud of saliva forming quietly in my moist mouth; I can very well sense its growing passion within. It seeks immediate attention, for it is excitedly willing to explode in at any moment, once reasonable approvable is granted. But my social conscience is in doubt. Though drowned in complete and recognised isolation, there has always been swamping in the heart of this woody wilderness, a worrisome possibility of youthful bikers unauthorisedly intruding this silent moment of personal bliss.

There in the depths of my dried-up mouth it persists in a fierce battle against the harsh weathers, forming a quiet union out of the newly accumulating swamp of neighbouring bodily waters and getting ready for the final explosion. A quiet and evolving rebellion was gradually drawing up in biological undergrounds. All it required was a vague node of approval.

But an unforeseen error keeps the agitating mob nail-bitingly suspended on the cliff-edge, desperately fighting for its freedom to bulge out into the mainstream in a heavy throw. A duality is draggingly brought to the front, the duality of the spit. Only it exists; nothing else.

And slowly, very smoothly, the duality splits itself peacefully into two equal slices like a perfectly slashed apple, and yeah, not even the tensed shattering of a porcelain mug was required for the power of choice to manifest its overtly displayable strength.

In the depths of the sun-pierced wild grasses, like transparent chemicals mutely blending with one another in a glassed test tube, sticky glittering saliva drooped drippingly from green to green: the choice had been made, the revolution ceased; it is time to go home now.

The will and the way are interlinked units of inspirational qualities.

The will and the way.

The will is the way.

The way is the will.

It is time to go home now.

Now.

Home.

Ho.

Sunday is the day dedicated to lost reflections in mystically lonesome strolls through the wilderness of Fern hill or wherever nearby affordable. Some weekdays too I go out for aimless wander, but they usually fall short and light, unmatchable to the intense dedication with which I calmly expect the day for acceptable idleness to arrive: Sunday is the day of monotonous freedom, of hard-earned leisure, of loudspeaker preaching and high-pitched devotional hymns.

"Self-contradiction is the first love of Sophia," "All the regrets in my life are somebody else's foolish cause," "If I die the world ceases; so is the case with you too. The post-credits kept rolling down in mute, dark screens; us and them mere passive audience," The show is over. Get lost or get home," - these are shortened summaries of few renderings from my previous Sunday stroll through the wilderness of Fern hill and beyond the lost late morning mists of Lovedale.

Indeed if I was the first man on earth, I should admit it would have been extremely laborious to place myself in space-time, or anywhere to be honest; only half-realised or semi-conscious takeaways, in the fortunate absence of common sense, would be my unrealised solace in those lonesome times. But what is life without brothers and fellow-men and women! The comforting yet disastrous sense of another is the sole cause of all evil on earth and in some mainstream parts of heaven too, I assume. It is manipulative; it is social, really unsocial, extremely dangerous, and it alone creates these endless paradoxes: this magnified, multiplied chaos is unfolding and originating from a deeply personal stream of very confidential yet common mysteries. I have become a changed man altogether.

Young men in biker suits and expensive gears perch themselves so proudly in roadside benches in the middle of Lovedale's calm wilderness. Their haughty faces reflect exhaustion and fatigue after a tireless ride all the way from down south. Royal motorbikes are parked elegantly near to their perched benches, as the group of tired, thoughtless bikers stare blankly into the depths of their respective personal cell-phones. A solitary walker pass by them uncaringly, disconnected and drawn, and I note with a touch of overwhelming fear their terrific stares that pierce through my morning senses like a butcher's slasher-knife.

Elsewhere, coral rocks stung in historic algae wetted in the irregular evening waves. It was an evening of simultaneous events and movements.

In no time the waves opened up and found themselves - their eternally moving identity, in the vague resemblances of a splendid anatomy of a microscopically analysed subject, one that evoked the curiosity of the laboratory-based biologist.

And in its turn the idealised consciousness too revealed simultaneously, incomprehensibly, mysteriously, unexplainably and relentlessly, barring itself in subjective prisons.

We are prisoners of subjectivity. Imprisoned by multiplied illusions and wardened by a conformist ego.

The eyes of a woman met the eyes of a man; for the split of a second that turned immeasurable in reflections, the moment of spiritual contact intertwined like woven fabric and finally locked in the passing connection of a chanced combination. The eyes of a woman met the eyes of a man or the eyes of a man met the eyes of a woman or both happened in irresistible simultaneity and that happened and that is that.

The world is celebrating in never-before-observed sophisticated manners, and here I am, statued like a roadside mannequin worn in dust and usual rush, overlooking the misty mountain lines now fading away with the setting sun. In this silent, dust-filled library containing the assorted glory of mankind, above an enormous framed portrait of Jean-Paul Sartre rests intellectually along with Goethe's and Mahatma Gandhi's; there is no room for any midnight celebrations or joyful feasts here tonight. Only quietness, transparent and evocative.

I read the continental philosophers, and I feel like ending this day like any other. But my good and acceptable outlooks and of all, the amplified rhymes emitting melodically from the valley church makes me to reunite with the celebrating crowd, with the people, with my own extended selves.

Eric Rohmer's Claire's Knees seems a good choice as a partial substitute for overt celebrations, for compromising, even though restrictively, this uninterrupted solitude with a slight touch of initiated external influences.

But in another moment I refrain myself in heeding to any societal obligations. Again and again I remind myself that I too am a laughable paradox, a mere reflection of eternal celebrations. What more is there to celebrate so merrily in a world of broken lights and shattered glasses? Where even budget hotels are occupied with greed and growing emptiness that morality needs to seek shelter elsewhere, to lodge on roadside cold compromises, confronting the cold winter with a torn blanket of smiling lies?

They have abruptly cut the speakers, no more music is transmitted, and none is to reach this otherwise. I am to sleep early tonight. Now that they too have concluded - or perhaps only halted for a deep breath brake, their annual celebrations, a little air of relief seems to have surrounded this room of deep calculations and conditionings. A wise man once told me that the mechanical tendency to cough is automatically aroused by your neighbour's continuous coughing.

Kids of the valley are expressing unconditioned joy in elated shouts; their innocent expressions of divinity too will be in time reduced to drab thickness by mechanical forces.

It is the day after the New Year celebration, the day when they replace outdated and used calendars with new and optimistic ones, when the white sheets of numbered futuristic days sway in the winds like fresh leaves, full of hope and determination.

By autumn, unfortunately or incidentally, the leaves turn pale and yellowish, no more inspirational or attractive, lacking confidence and security.

The sleepy hour of last nights' when I drearily wrote the above solitary words was New Year Eve. A conditioned and ready-made one.

I walk the streets with a returning migraine, expecting lavish street photographs. But I end up wonderingly standing, motionless, in front of a lonesome statue right in the middle of a screeching square. There are people all around; the streets are occupied, there is nowhere else to run to, nobody to share few passing words with. Nobody knows where they are going, but somehow all seem to find their way back home.

Harsh winds blow, knocking at the glass doors rigorously. It is a belief-worn sign. An ancient, clichéd one. Something dreadful is to happen today. At the least, something or the other *ought* to happen. For it is the historic, celebrated reality after all that is being played house-full and full of ambitions, concerns and sorrow.

At this moment, at the onset of this eternal wave in heavy splashing, I was unfastening the half-corroded metal bolt. The door has been securely locked and insane leafy shadows are casted on varnished plywood.

Faint, harmless shadows are being reflected on the foggy glasses, and fiercely, the slender wild plants beat the blemished glasses in accordance to the rhythmic winds that shed its overwhelming mark like the oily hair of a native woman. It is a bright, windy day and I don't know what I am doing on this rowdy earth, or wherever I have been magically placed. It is the day of lostness. Wild melodies of limited freedom have already started beating. Something is to happen. Something is waiting occasionally, either in hung-over streets or lonely woods. Perhaps these heavy winds may even bring ordinary rains. Only God knows.

As usual, nothing happens. Through these hung-over parties of streets and funeral lanes highly contagious with deadly diseases and reviving from midnight dances did a lost man infected with life walk in raised wisdom, loaded fully with abundant freedom and youth.

Two young lovers, full of energy and passion, walked past him, hand in hand, and only then did the short and clean-shaven wisdom-carrier find some relief and breathing space and thereby released the sticky aspect of his consciousness from the agonising smell of rotten eatables emitting continually from the wasted grounds. He tilted and slowly turned back his tired head and saw glimpses of freedom, wild innocence and certain aspects of his own untamed days fading away in the crowded distance of elongated blurriness. The lovers walked hand in hand; perhaps their divided psychological dimensions too mingled in similar manners. Maybe the former must have been an apt and co-incidental correspondence analogy for the mysterious sublimity of the intermingling.

To conclude and thereby find rhythm with this everlasting lostness that keep now and then imposing its own presence to the mainstream, I may, with all due respect, provoke an ancient and long-forgotten word - something that'll surely stir the comfortably harmonised minds of mainstream syncronity, one of brotherly conformity.

CHAPTER SIX

I AM OR AM-ING

Since this short prose manuscript has been written in first person, let me pull and straighten-up all my accumulated income to strip myself away and perhaps try and grasp a little what this reduced semanticist essentially stands for, if at all for anything or nothing or something.

If the phenomenal is a mere extension of your inner, how can you go in without first submerging yourself in the exterior? Henri Bergson speaks so elegantly about how the colour orange would exist on its own had its partner shades, red and yellow, never been revealed. In such an unrevealed hypothetical situation, the shade orange would be stripped of its "yellowness" and "redness"; not even in the "virtual" or "hypothetical", according to Bergson.

So is the case with us - humane species indefinitely pregnant with reality and slippery objects of untraceable origin and multiplicity, too - helplessly normalised and conditioned out of sheer necessity and practical applications. If not for the phenomenal, one wouldn't ponder over the imaginary, or the inner, and conduct such in-depth analysis or phenomenological studies. In the prior absence of one, the question of "another" wouldn't substantiate itself in the first place; unity may not stand alone without its implied multiplicity already evident and inherent in the former's linguistic versatility. This is phenomenal, it is a fact. So is the experiential existence of the inner, for even these words are derived from it. One may be the other, and vice versa. But, anyhow, if not for the mild, irrevocable separation, that and this and all of it including the indefinable concept of nothingness would mingle into an inseparable whole that is denied unmindful of both multiplicity and unity or the two contained and co-existent in full freedom and interdependence like mutually-beneficial friends.

The phenomenal is true and acceptable, alright, but its existential validity pertains to reducible falseness.

Thank goodness there is a clear cut distinction between the phenomenal and the other, whatever they are or that is.

Indian mystique Narayana Guru speaks methodically about such dualities persistent and substantial even in higher, transcendental realms. In no way is the contemporary man of modernised preferences imaginable of travelling such heights.

But there is another interesting, highly innovative conception. It is of the oscillating consciousness, one that, like a fluttering bee, keeps moving to and fro in the presence of things and states - basically, itself, producing images and ideas and perceptions from the thing as a being and the idea of the thing. It is this highly mystical concept we are concerned about here.

Where there is movement, spatial differences prevails. So too is the inner space here that keeps twisting and bending in accordance to the free flow of consciousness. For how are movements perceived if not translated to spatial extensiveness.

For Bergson, experiencing reality in its purity is the immediate knowledge of things and other such discourses, physiological or psychological. A lot of fluttering and drama is involved and contained in flowing unison in such a simple act as that of an immediate perception.

Here builds up the deceptive reality of the one who perceives. Greatly narcissistic as it may sound, for me it has been myself alone for a very long time indeed; not relative, but purely deductible and bohemian.

Jean-Paul Sartre in the "Transcendence of the Ego," refers it to be something as revealable (I don't really remember reading this or writing it down. But now that I am editing this text almost two years later, I convince myself of the exceptional qualities of my memory and try to find existential certitude in it, how much ever thrusted it may be in subjectively psychological realms of self-assurance).

In contrast, it is always there, it is all pervading. This much celebrated I is rather a lie. A simple yet weird one. A relative paradox. Something of a well-sought deception. One knows the truth, and one knows very well that he is concealing it, and yet he earnestly reveals the false, or the partial truth, to the other.

This other is we. It is the I which is the concealed lie. It is there all right for easy grabs, yet it so wonderfully, like thrown banana peels in already slippery floors, evades our firm footings. It is I and it is not.

The reflective I is but a roadside reflection, or a summertime shadow. Even in reflective moments, the I slips through our gentle hands prankfully. For in the act of reflection, we are merely reflecting on the I, and not in itself.

Through busy street lanes we wander foolishly; in lonesome woods I stroll solitarily; on the pale wooden desk I place both my hands over my cheeks in thoughtful reflections. Yet that I am in search of evades me, the I that we consciously seek evades itself, I evade myself, in the moments of our earnest efforts, and yet absurdly it is me, for it is I who is earnestly reflecting. It can be placed and it cannot and should not and it refuses to be placed. Yet it is it and this and that and what not and it-is-not too.

The moment is endured: a very simple and straightforward act.

What is incomprehensible, inexplainable, expensive, indefinable or even mysterious or novel and free, can whatsoever be represented, however vaguely or indefinitely, in linguistic platforms or mathematical outlines translated to words.

And let me put forward frankly, when was the last time space was equipped with a stand-alone position? Aren't the material objects and matter in itself the space they are co-related and correspond to like an inseparable relation? And qualitative impressions, deep and mysterious, are sublimely imposed onto fogs of spatial dullness, transforming it altogether in essence and thereby equipping it with a deep and heavenly transcendental grace in reflections. For if not reflected upon reality curiously and attentively, it may perhaps evade you and may even overspeed itself out of silly sentiments arising of the negligence. Either ways, both the fact, the proof, the stability of the occurrence and the ultimate result is transcendence, pure, natural, on-its-own or deliberate.

It is similar to the mixed fruit of jam of pineapples and apples. If not attentively abstracted, you never get to know which one is what. And if not properly abstracted, the mixed fruit-jam exists as a mixed fruit-jam of pineapples and apples, simple, jelly and tasty.

The mixed fruit-jam existence.

As it is, so to speak, is there a substantial need for abstraction if the mixed fruit-jam available in front is simple, jelly and tasty in the first place? What is that stir and the ache in the heart of the satisfied eater that relentlessly provokes this aggressive forward march of unstoppable abstraction if the taste buds have already been satisfied and content? Of all, as it is, that underlying enjoyer too, comprising of the enjoyable and the very act of enjoyment itself.

Let us pause and think again for a moment. If the I is all-inclusive, why does it need a shelter? And why should it be sought? There lies a mild mystery. Perhaps it is not the I we seek after all. For that which we seek is already within our own stretchful reach. The I is here in the absence of our reflection, in the presence of it, in all our struggle and happiness and whatsoever, yet is remains a lie. A mirage, or a photoshopped image.

From above to below the line is drawn. From downstairs the same line is sought by the curious caveman of smartphone torchlight. From above to below transcendence takes hold of itself in full freedom or loneliness, finding and losing itself in unearthed, simultaneous multiplicity of the ontological garages.

A lonesome railway station of the hills. It is cold and foggy. One train moves and the other does not. Beyond the relative discrepancies, the two trains move harmoniously in underlying unison of contained simultaneity. Where movements collapse, the trains themselves become irrelevant or in them alone significance register itself in winged perceptions.

Oh, the lonely benches of hill stations; they are faded, reflected and creeper-filled. Benches of hill stations.

Most often, what inspires the eye and what the ears listen do not match or correspond with one another, though they are diverse simultaneities of the same ongoing run. These broken bits of reality is, in fact, what is most often in absent practical applications - where reflective judgements stand suspended, given as the ongoing reality of life, what is moulded and punched into a baked bread of sorrows and dread.

Most of what appeals to the mind as bizarre or absurd or other-than-usual are caused mostly externally, often in your neighbour or brother or a passenger-train stranger. Say, the strangers are introduced and they get along well, their specific subjective minds mingle and synchronise, and the former happens to be a conformist citizen and the barely processed idea already strikes as strange or rather unusual. Years pass-by, the earth keeps revolving but is terribly exhausted and heated up and the days are shorter and warmer and the trends are recycled and the winds blow repeatedly and the train of chance-encounters are modified, serviced and made perfectly adaptable to the then prevailing standards of living and you have matured. You are a grown man now, settled and systematic and have over the years evolved, listened, reflected and witnessed yourself change and flex and become a believer and, obviously, it is perfectly alright to be one now.

And at the end of the day I alone triumphs. We are saved, reduced and sustained by this subjectively collective ego that is so versatile, adaptive and many a times negative and flawed but alright and manageable from the point of view of a long-term vision.

The existentialist exceedingly stressed on the often overlooked supremacy of this all-in-all or overall consciousness, for what escapes it, in fact, escapes it in itself, and as itself. Thereby, subjective transcendence become apparent: transcendence of the subject from the mistaken vision of the filtered-out ego to that of the hierarchical, fully developed version of the I, complete, total and sufficient in itself: how often have we mistaken the comic imitator of the actor to be the veteran actor himself?

That which we really seek in our loneliest hours is and am the I and beyond the I. But the beyond too, efficiently, nobly, peacefully, contained and wrapped within the trans-subjective envelopes of the cosmic psyche; something that will escape us forever, something that is inexpressible and inaccessible, something that is me; extensions of reality, here to there.

Yet, in all its entirety and great mysterious nature, it is me alone that I seek; I escape myself: yet it is I that am. Not a reflective revelation or an aesthetic mask, but a simple lie. One ought to even the grounds before sowing the fields. The fatigued, piled-up ego that we are is nothing but a common flu, a spatial myth, acquired in the short, evolutionary run, and who knows, even easily transmittable. It holds a lot of promises, it is here, within us, in and as us, yet forever on the run, like an infamous outlaw or a dangerous fugitive. However, inexplicably, in the long run, the dedicated policeman and the great fugitive mingles, becoming one grand conspiracy.

Repetition is novelty.

Something that baffles me, arrests my immediate inner surroundings - a brief glimpse of which makes me shiver, is the understanding of the understanding. Why should I be installed with such a highly expensive and intellectual faculty? Why am I able to reflect on existence in teashops, tapioca fields and pastime reveries? How am I able to speak so clearly about the muddled and muddy atmosphere of my own self? Of all, how did such a curious and historic notion of a mystery, a certain something of the beyond or the beyond come to be in the first place? Am I or am I-ing?

As for now, it is too foggy everywhere; very obscured and impenetrable for our mild, listless gazes. If I am to gaze upon the original landscapes concealed behind this great fog, I need to venture out. In the casual stroll I think and I reflect. And finally I reach a decent vantage point from where I can at the least spot the beautiful trees and hills far away that were earlier veiled by the fog. Yet I can only look upon, perhaps even stare, and not become one among the widespread beauty. Always a distant spectator, the real beauty escapes me. Yet I see, I witness, and I endure.

1. 10. 2021. Two years after the first draft of this work was completed and five days after my birthday I start editing this particular chapter and realised how overtly ambitious I was then. A lot of what has been written is complete blunder but I still go about with it, for at least certain points hold good. Today I would like to restate and alter myself and assert the extensitivity of the I: from ontology to epistemology and back again it swirls, sways and oscillates within its own remarkable intensity in the likes of a virtual ball trapped in the closed loop of a 90's Microsoft game board. Please accustom yourself with an intellectual filter before completely digesting whatever has been noted down in this particular chapter.

In the midst of autumn it rained outside. The slightly slanted rain-sticks fell harshly. Build within the four sides of the rectangular bars of the window, a relatively new and modern cobweb swayed and danced in uncontrollable joy, a marvellous celebration of the coming of the rains. Resembling a neatly laid-out fishing nets in a coastal town, the soft and whitish cobweb displayed swift and smooth curves like the celebrated moves of a thrilled dancer.

I believe I am forced to write novels, to restrict myself to factious environments, just because I cannot find any other medium to express what I have been lately experiencing in blindfolded ecstasy.

A loose tooth in the sole of a broken shoe; my brownish leather shoe. Did I mention about it before? - About the psychedelic and unbearable toothache of my torn leather shoe? - A guest appearance.

A tale of addictive toothaches and torn leather shoes.

CHAPTER SEVEN

MARGINALS & SIDE NOTES

Imagination freezes the phenomenal; either one outstrips the other in that bizarre ceaseless marathon run of consciousness' from one pole to the other, as the great reformer-mystique so magnificently conceives it from his deeply mystical absorptions.

Often the daily-life mind stumbles upon something, a thought, a random occurrence, or even a hateful memory, and plunges deep into its interiors. Further seems inconceivable, as gradually the idea loses its potency and fades away into the void, leaving the mind frozen, which in its delicate representation in the world of images appeal to be gazing absently into the abstract depths of a pinkish soap container resting on a broken windowsill and the light green leaves gleaming splendidly in the regular daytime rains beyond the wooden windows.

There is a freezing point in each reminiscent glory where even the faintest recollections disintegrates and collapses into the abyss of no end, and the phenomenal world is slowly brought up from the darkest corners while absent gazes dissolve and give way to the sudden entry of logic.

When actively attending one of the morning classes did a swollen echo from the past flash by me in great magnitude, submerging my attentive world altogether. But, as revealed in later initiated throwbacks, that sudden flash of troubling memories seem to overpower all the splendid and cosy images available from the tranquil room of worship. It was either the flashing memories or the charming beard, a nice inner bargain.

It is then I decided to dedicate a separate session as a means of easy disposal for these occasional and abrupt reveries and pastime words which have no relative relevance in any structural context. As they keep coming so shall they be stockpiled until the burning pot overflows.

CHAPTER EIGHT

CARELESS DAYS

Unbrushed kisses, uncombed curly hairs, denim jeans' undone and philosophical concepts barely understood, those were wild days, full of youth and enriched phenomenology. Heavenly and unreflective, we were driven solely on pure innocence, on the savage motorbikes of our underdeveloped becoming. Through the sunshine shores we strolled dreamingly, man behind woman, hung-over by last night's cold sleep by the breezy beach. And we were careful enough to be driven by our own personal playlists, contemporary blues for her and soft rock for me. Yet our varying tastes somehow united in some distinct harmony that reverberated passionately in our shared tension. It was the longing for freedom, for the ideal home, lavish money, acres of green, and a shared, personal time. All the so-called impossible and crazy are the most deeply felt and endured, virtually in the least.

When the woodcutter of the valley fulfils his inescapable existential project in great dedication, the sounds of his craft echo wonderfully through the neighbouring woods and in the stillness of the hills. Somewhere in the depths of a transcendental island or a shatterproof earth must be traced, like lonesome weeds sprouting unceasingly maintained by their own creativity, all the cringe-worthy moments and socially careless stains of these bygone carefree days. In such a spiritual belief I move on being in the solitary wrecks of youthful madness. All the worlds and the heavens and the post-credits belong to pure youthful lust. They belonged to us; to me and her, and to the great many or the wild wild many temporary lovers these makeshift soil was blessed with.

It is a common human tendency to animate another's weakness and lodge in it like an yesteryear creeper. And that exactly was what happened between us. But until then, every dealing was direct and underground, the earthly and the heavenly interwoven like a handloom bag. In many a drowsy sunrise in the awakening shores of Bessie beach, heaven came down and assumed the grand, bluish vastness with the horizon and the sunrise waters. There aren't much synonyms at disposable, in languages or in life, to exactly translate the other-worldly feelings that excessive visions often carry along with the soothing winds. But we experienced it on a shared moment that transcended time or stood superior to it, something contemporarily often carelessly and vaguely referred to as love. It is good, most often its intensity depends majorly on seasons and varying moods or relativity and rarely on intellectual intimacy.

It must definitely have been a full moon day, for that comprised with others, a major reason for the first kiss, the most tensed one of all. Hanging at the farther end of the cool beach lane like an old woman's pierced ears, that coincidental full moon favoured us in our confused tendencies that warm breezy evening we thoughtlessly decided to take our growing whispers to the mainstream yet serene beach. One by one when the evening crowd, mostly families and frequent youth, left, we excitedly waved goodbyes to the world and its responsibilities, as we spend the night in passionate kisses under the thin cover of the native fishermen's fishing boats - firm nets in proper places and all set to go for tomorrow's great hunt. Half-exposed to our first-night moonlight and to the bare seas, our inexperienced palms in each other's chests, we gazed upon the signs of cosmic wonder bursting incredibly on the dark, lustful skies of our immature ecstasy. We were young and cruel, all our senses and thoughts were overflowing with temptations, but we were guarded by the elderly sympathy of the divine grace on our sprouting conscience. So do I like to reflect upon it now, and no poet is willing to correct me on the same.

But from then on a mutual awkwardness grew between us, whose psychological wings seemed longer than the classroom space we once pleasantly shared. Time does heal, if not regretful scars, at least the gentle wounds of its own carcasses, for we set out again, afresh and thrilled, and we intensely mingled our young, fresh lips, this time not in nightly shores but in sun-soaked waters of our poetic Bessie. When we returned from the saline beach shore waters, mildly intoxicated in cheap coastal rum or ultra-strong brandy, our wet hands had on their own established a firm grip, and we, for brief moments, walked composedly over time, lost in ecstasy, lost beyond being, yet time and time again falling within its own irresistibly vast and indefinite frontiers. We were uncertified lovers, following the scenic and irregular footsteps of freelance photographers. We didn't know what we were, yet we had a social designation - free and unpaid lovers. She whispered melodies of adorable resonance, and in return, her pinkish, apple-like cheeks wetted and became sticky in showers of unwanted kisses. Either of us was plain old school, but in time we lost track of our own gradual dawning; outlines of pathetic childhood days or of past lives were mystically retraced only as laughable reminiscences in drunken happy moods or ordinary evening awkwardness.

Feeling awkward at being. Just 90's things.

For me nothing is more bizarre and strangely than this whole business of a flowing, unceasing reality, a bit over-speeding at times, most often incomprehensible and reckless and truly unbelievable when reflected upon. And what exactly is this reflecting upon! Placed in oneself and reflecting upon its own mysteriously weird incomprehensible tendencies. One thing I know that I am aware and this awareness is me and it opens up and spreads its wings like a wild creeper and this is real and the real is meditated upon from the unreal and words are spilled thrills, intellectual and deep.

When precisely did the tragic downfall of our epic romance commence - I cannot really recall, but I do remember riding dejectedly with a heavy heart through the vast highways of our lost love, totally clueless of the correct deviations to take, or how many more kilometres to ride and fuel tanks to exhaust before the final and overwhelming burnout.

It must have been that nasty encounter with the ruthless cops in the brilliantly lit highways of East Coast Road, or perhaps it was the ugly experience with some youngsters in the drunken streets of Bessie that ransackingly revealed the shivering, compressed forms of my truer selves, so far hiding so comfortably in the thick blankets of my tough, "young man" outlook.

No, it shouldn't be all that. Definitely not. In the heart of the chance glance at the complex corridors of tensed entrance examinations in the beginning of a tremendous summer itself did she effortlessly strip my psyche bare naked and closely observe the weird formations and structural malfunctions.

Reason may find no working grounds to dig painstakingly in great deserts in search of logical waters. It is always better to cherish the blissful and orgasmic than the rotten, the latter quite often available in plenitude. If not, one may just take a quick drive through the storeroom of one's own immediate or recent memories.

Let me not go there. Not tonight, when my valley neighbours are drinking in the relieving finale of a heavy year. And I can wave a solitary farewell to this honourable night like most days, in the proud certitude that tonight she is thinking of none but me, of no other absurd highways but mine, for the troublesome presence of no one but my very own, broken and troubled. I can sign a happy closure to this lonesome night when all my peers will be drinking to good health with that mild tinge of uncertainty. Only a selected few remember me, care for me, and I am forever thankful for that. To whomsoever it may concern.

A genuine meditation of the moment is what is required to transcend logic. For there is a justifiable reason for the piercing reflection of sun-rays on transparent waters of the evening hours to conduct a full blast on your eyes. Nonetheless it is a moment of true idleness that would reveal the real content - the sun-rays reflected on the waters. The rest is add-ons by the faculty of imagination or that poor frustrated ego of one's troubled upcoming, strugglingly striving to cut slices of meaning out of the all-embracing knowledge cake, creamy and unexplained.

In late springs and prolonged winters I was able to find myself and relate my conscious existence in remembrance to lonesome benches more than anything else, more than my own rendered and bruised image reflected spontaneously on hanging mirrors. Strong and resolute, careless bees flew around its meditative stillness in replenished childishness. Yet, unheeding to movements and conditions, the granite bench, craved and beaten, stood still and unbothered by the winds and the tides, against purposeful gazes and occasional glances.

Lonesome benches of Bessie and the Nilgiris, short and flat and deep.

Almost four years ago, on the eve of a similar but not so lonesome New Year Eve, we sped moderately with bewildered, sleep-filled eyes through vast highways of side-lined men and party-minded youths, all cracking fireworks and dancing heartily like drunken heroes. All in the mood for heavy celebrations, we wanted a nice and cosy elitist room for the night to be wasted on tight hugs and, perhaps, a bit of soft rock explosion. And yes, a lot of cigarettes, of course. Preferably, those that bursts to flavoured tastes. Thus we too welcomed the upcoming paper calendars by bursting Dunhills and kissing cinematically until one of us involuntarily submitted to deep-sleep. But deep into the night, one of us, or rather a weak portion of our shared psychology, exhaled a missing-out feeling, a kind of bacterial aching of the ego-teeth, and we set out with extremely sleepy eyes back to the world of celebrations, to be shivering helplessly in the merciless blowing of cold, coastal winds.

Amidst all the evolving crowds, great struggles and pleasures, all the vanishing images and newly emerged ones, amongst rainy nights and darkened walks and soul-seeking and ambitious pondering, selfish detachments and indifference, it is a painstaking task to find one's own true bearings. And in fleeting romances and brilliant love chats I saw glimpses of some relief. When all the tender whispers and freezing philosophies diminished in the dark, like a fluttering vagabond bird in search of some transparent waters, I, in brief seasonal moments that lay mild resemblances to bimonthly comics, finally got in terms with my own rainy self, fresh and historical, wet and dripping, mingled in flowing mud on dampened grounds. "This is life. This is existence. This is great," we simultaneously spoke aloud in silenced embraces in the expense of intense spaces of our shared personal psychology. Which was whose, and who was whose, only stagnant memories could distinguish. Varying dense colours burst gaily in the coastal skies, cracking and sparkling, marking the immediate happening of another long-awaited man-made year. It is the time for collective celebrations, drunken or whatever.

We spend the celebration night shivering in the sandy shores, wetted, wasted and utterly uncomfortable. The only solace to pass the night in some relief was the crystal fact that sometime in retrospection, this night would be stamped thrustingly with a melancholic smile, analytically certified as an inexperienced rigour of original, wonderstruck urges.

In the morning we woke up to slightly embarrassed yawns, and in another year or so, after great unfamiliar hassles and much family interference, we got married peacefully in a low, vernacular house of prayer, a country church faraway from burning industrial toxics. Happy new-born kids were raised in another year. But, unfortunately, out of nowhere that has its certifiable origin in subjective psychology, deep and blurred, extraneously furnished insecurities and deceptive restlessness unexpectedly got hold of me, and I took my leave in an economy class ticket on an international flight, to faraway burning seas of oil and high towers, in search of wealth and life's immoral pleasures, abandoning - completely in negligence, of what was once so dear and eternal and promised forever. The indispensable, enlightening image of Deepa Paulose is as dear and favoured by my memories as the immediate clippings of immediate realities sticking around in bits and slices of the regrets of yesterday, the calm stillness of today and the obscured uncertainties of tomorrow. I hope to reunite with her someday, in this animated enhancement or the ones yet to come.

CHAPTER NINE

EPILOGUE TO INDIFFERENCE

Other than life, any extraneous habits, acquired or otherwise, should be completely avoided. It is a well-wisher's advice. If not, one may tend to float in indifferent waves, pale and shivering. Whatever you do - the worst may yet to happen, never be a misfit for life.

In fact and sensible reflections, the first statement is self-contradictory.

One after the other, seasons get postponed, majorly due to expert reasons. Penetrating even the thick shields of reality-beaten skins and bones, the tremendous winters of Fern-hill and Lovedale makes even the most cautious, the most reflective ones - gone exceedingly too far in his courageous drive to the impenetrable bottom of becoming, get his cracking palms burn in the smoky waters of a fuming geyser. It is a moment of extreme accelerations; time shifts gears so rapidly, so hastily, as though a wild elephant has been unexpectedly spotted in the long, great uphill drive. Sensitive hands burned and soft red; cracked and roaring. Moments overflowing, no more time to reflect, only few spare parts to act with. A rare sensation, sudden and quite natural, trips our beloved idler, the great pretender of reflections and prophecies, to his own sneezy nose, on his own personal cheekiness. But, as many great loneliness has mild silences and reflections as a sort of prerequisite, as all precious memories have a dearer owner, this sudden sensation too has its own installed counterparts. When all the appalling alarms and cries receded down to wakeful thoughts, this moment too had a small room generously allotted for analysis or basic intellectual activities, whatever: to have been burned by a completely novel flowing stream of hot waters, and instant, instinctive treatments with proper care and basic hospitality, and of all, and for a very uncommon, remarkable sensation to be immediately revoked, in a flash of a second, if one may, the revoker - that is the fuming running water, and the revoked sensation, should have a cream-like prior, concurrent, parallel or simultaneous existence in a tranquil state; squashed and indistinguishable. How much ever a boiled egg is dug deep into an egged and overcooked rice-meal, it so smoothly, effortlessly, rises above all the great crafty pressures by a simple, elegant and compassionate touch of its master's ravenous hands.

With such and such ongoing trials, seasons and episodes, this and that and this-ness and that-ness and something-ness, one may be affirmatively tended to conclude that there is life on earth, whatever it may tend to be. There are experiences, and great fleeting moods. And of all, there is immeasurable beauty in them, for all of the above are extensions, brilliantly laid out like an expanded rubber band; they are never once, for then they should already have been. Sometimes, in the midst of these orderly chaos and foolish marathon races, there is a high chance for mind to get lost or misplaced somewhere in the mad order of its own messy, shrunken-down corridors. And when one, in a busy cabdriver's impatient waiting and an authoritative boss' blazing calls, is to hurriedly come back for the missing mind in that same old thatched hut room, two or more classic novels may easily be displaced, a dozen of vowels wonderfully misplaced, and a procession of superstitious rats crazily pacing through the cracked walls like Spiderman's prodigal sons. But nowhere will the lost mind be explicitly displayed in the resemblances of a framed portrait, for in the depths of sailing time it had already made a divine promise, and in virtue of its noble history, it shall forever abide to the old man's gainful laws: it had long, long time ago drowned sorrowfully in a ravageous indifferent monsoon.

Fruitful application of intellectual successiveness to objective simultaneities give the latter its mobile identity.

Or is there a mysterious force, a divine Olympic runner, divinely unifying the inner to the without in its spellbound and inexplainable mobility?

Intellect's qualitative input in the form of ceaseless, gripping mobility.

The I takes a massive U-turn in terms of Mother Nature. And the untraceable and forever-widening curve indefinitely separates us from physics.

There are days. There is a Sunday. Individuals reverentially attend holy masses. Like a rigid bridge tremulously hanging overhead a magnificently flowing river, a compositional separation in the carpeted middle clearly peels a distinction.

There is a bus-stop, a shack-like one, in a secluded overgrown junction, and there is a vague idea of an incoming bus. Two bus waiters or future passengers, one young and searchive, the other done and passive, stand close to each other in stony fashions, in mild hostility quite common to everyday strangers. In their silent wait, old age mingles with rigorous haziness, and one becomes another, and vice versa. Slowly the fading evening reveals signs of arrivals and departures, the end of an era of a day and the coming of its dialectical wife. It is the mark of the end of a heavy, working day. Streetlight reflections spilled on muddy rain waters sparkle so profoundly, and daily-wage working women in colourful, vibrant plastic raincoats walk back home, laughingly, contently. A confused dog wanders lousily; a shivering man goes to the tiny stationary shop opposite to the rectangular half-opened box-like bus stop, and the aimless dog follows him with deep respect. Then another man, this time a retired professor it must be, strolls pleasantly through the detached, unpopulated wet roads, merrily appreciating nature and enduring life, and the wandering dog immediately leaves behind his momentary infatuations one after the other and goes behind another. In the autobiography of a French philosophical writer, he sits existentially in a European bus, waiting for some kind of revelation, as he has been for almost all his life. Confusion, exposed weakness, unpublished restlessness, attempted glories, scattered priorities, great happiness, greater indifference, unsurpassable artistic urges, a vague introduction to the arrival of night has been artistically displayed in the dimming skies of dark, flashback clouds. For a handful few, nightfall is a creative dawn. And in that moment of abundant realities and pure waiting, eternity so smoothly went by unnoticed. At certain specific waitful moments of unintentional reflection-strikes, eternity seem so less, so cute. Life is not absurd; the very fact that one is living is, however subjective it may sound.

As time went on, ever-new stuffs got continuously introduced into the systematic, orderly reality.

On cracking walls of whitewashed bricks dropping ancient clocks in slow-motion tick endlessly, mercilessly, always constant, even when the end of time melodically approaches.

Autumnal leaves clicked and flickered in the air, echoing the clicking hands of fibre weaving artisans. I was monumentalised in the midst of a quietly clicking autumn, in between everlasting seasons and a southern ego.

Somewhere in between the rusty railroads of the Nilgiri's far-reaching stretch of thickly populated wilderness, and through the cool and uninhibited multi-layered plantations of the countryside, I lost and later revived my mind. Many years later, in the magnificent splash of a split of a second, I found it hanging securely on silhouetted trees, transparent cobwebs, alien-looking fishing nets, vintage rear-view windows, free highway rides or even in the depths of a soft nightmare. So far, so here. For the real meanings locked within gets influenced easily. After all, it's a child at heart.

From a soft whistling breeze to a thunderstruck wave, the real, freer self survived, adapted, improvised and enhanced itself from within and without, from above and so, beyond, in the tremendously sharpened visions of an Indian mystique or the meditatively transcendental progression of an English hard rock song. Seasons swept; they harvested bliss, and freedom sprung from open grounds, fresh and lively and full of hope.

9 798885 553612

Printed by Libri Plureos GmbH in Hamburg,
Germany